Alex and K(

Seatopia

Book 2: The Eye of Odin
By
David J. Wimer

DOUBLE DRAGON PUBLISHING

The Eye Of Odin
Copyright © 2017 David J. Wimer

Double Dragon Press

An Imprint of
Double Dragon Publishing
PO Box 54016
1-5762 Highway 7 East
Markham, Ontario L3P 7Y4 Canada
http://www.double-dragon-ebooks.com
http://www.double-dragon-publishing.com

ISBN-13: 978-1546745556
ISBN-10: 1546745556

A DDP First Edition May 16, 2017
Book Layout and
Cover Art by Deron Douglas

★

This book is dedicated to Todd, Allison, and Bartleby.

"We have not even to risk the adventure alone
for the heroes of all time have gone before us.
The labyrinth is thoroughly known
we have only to follow the thread of the hero path.
And where we had thought to find an abomination
we shall find a God.

And where we had thought to slay another
we shall slay ourselves.
Where we had thought to travel outwards
we shall come to the center of our own existence.
And where we had thought to be alone
we shall be with all the world."

-Joseph Campbell

Chapter 1

Life begins in water. Floating in the warm, inviting comfort of your mother's womb. Seeds of existence swimming through sustaining fluid with a scintillant hope of continuity; primordial life penetrating the surface to embrace a sandy shore.

The blood pumping through your body originates from sea water and the rains of antiquity. Now in the 22nd century this life giving liquid enshrouds an accumulative portion of the world's surface, and wealthier humans have retreated to the womb-like bubble cities beneath the waves with their brethren left behind on the wounded, imbalanced land.

The serene water surrounding the Seatopia city of New Richmond flows in a perpetual rhythm, but a sudden *explosion* breaks the serenity – and a battle rages around the city.

Unified attack subs surge toward New Richmond with their weapons blazing. Seatopia sub drones (small, sleek trapezoids with glowing red eyes) send pulse cannons percolating through the water to meet them in a parley of aggression.

Lamborghini-like Enclave subs stream through the Atlantic sending volleys of laser torpedoes, turning many of the drones into bubbling husks, as the drones take down their share of attacking subs. Several sub drones converge on a Unified vessel to bombard it with cannon blasts, disabling the force shield to make frothing rents in the hull until one of them finishes the job with a torpedo. Manta ray-like submarines from the Marine Emergency Reactive Military Aid unit pour into the fray to blast drones at will. A few stray torpedoes slam into the crumbling, sunken ruins of Old Richmond. Weapons fill the once peaceful water and the seabed becomes an ever increasing ship graveyard.

The Unified fleet blasts an opening in the swarming wall of sub drones to surge past them toward the waiting bubble dome. The first wave of Unified subs, however, slams into a portcullis of invisible depth charges around the city – causing a cascade of bubbling explosions and heavy casualties. The detonating charges phase into appearance for a split second before disappearing again. The fleet falls back in response to this unexpected setback, forced into a standoff with the pesky drones.

Marcus Taylor races through the water in a brand new, single pilot fighter sub that looks like a sleek, slightly tilted crescent moon. Marcus sees the depth charges flash for a split second on the midair holographic display in his cockpit, and looks ahead through the viewport to see fellow soldiers die in the waste. Their crippled subs sink to the bottom leaving bubbles in their wake. Raymond Kildare streams right behind him in his own fighter sub and says into his earpiece, "Damn, they must have known we were coming. Wasn't this supposed to be a *sneak* attack?"

"Someone or something must have tipped them off. Do you see anything that might be cloaking the charges?"

"Not right now. We need to get closer to the city, but it's going to be damn hard. We need Miranda and her team in the water ASAP."

Marcus quickly sends the message to Miranda's command sub, but doesn't have time to think after that: a host of Seatopia drones turn their attention to the new fighter subs and fill the deep liquid with pulse cannon blasts. Marcus, Ray, and the other fighter pilots break off in a defensive pattern to evade fire while returning fire of their own. Marcus picks off a few drones and maneuvers away from enemy shots with expert precision. Ray moves his fighter swiftly through the water, loving how well these new subs maneuver, and concentrates on blasting drones before they hit his comrades. The small sub drones only have one torpedo each, like a bee with a lone stinger, but a few of them release their torpedoes before being blown to smithereens. The enemy laser torpedoes destroy a few Unified fighter subs, making the suddenly lifeless shells spin through the water, while two more torpedoes tail Ray's sub like rats behind the Pied Piper. Marcus turns from his target to blast one of the torpedoes streaking toward his friend. Ray operates countermeasures with a wave of his lone hand. A defensive pulse shoots out to destroy the torpedo and the resultant blast wake sends Ray's fighter tumbling through the bubbling liquid until he can reclaim his bearings to fight afresh.

Dr. Brendan Kim sits wearing his trademark lab coat in the command chair of the *Myrmidon,* the M.E.R.M.-Aid unit's large flagship that's crisscrossed inside by water-filled tubes so the aquatic soldiers can freely traverse the ship in their natural form, when he receives the signal from Marcus's fighter sub. He turns to Lieutenant Colonel Miranda Ulmo, the aquatic soldier leader who also happens to be the love of his life, and says, "It's time. Marcus and Ray need you out there."

Miranda answers by walking up, giving him a deep kiss, and saying, "Make sure you have a fresh bucket of fish ready for me when I get back." She runs her hand along his arm before her countenance turns businesslike as she rotates to face her soldiers. She doesn't flinch when the *Myrmidon* is rocked by a laser blast hitting the force shield. Miranda fires up her soldiers with a nod and a grin of bloodlust. They follow her into the pool and out to the lockout trunk with their weapons ready; the aquatic soldiers *live* for combat.

Miranda, Major Shelly Naiad, Major Lisa Cardita, Captain Margot Unagi, Lieutenant Ariel Triton, and the rest of the M.E.R.M.-Aid unit stream into the water to meet the onrushing drones. They plow through the water with swishes of their powerful tails as they fire their pulse cannons at any drone within range. Miranda and the others deftly weave around enemy fire while laying waste to the sub drones, and they are so agile that they take few casualties.

New Richmond launches manned attack subs to reinforce the drones – cylindrical gray ships similar to the Pharmadyne subs at the Battle of New Charlotte. The *Myrmidon* and other Unified ships turn their attention to these newcomers with the usual barrage of torpedoes and pulse blasts.

Meanwhile, Dr. Prapti Gupta sits in the command chair on the *Virginia's* bridge, giving orders and focusing on the intricacies of underwater combat. The ship has taken some hits but the force shield is holding. Kristin Thatcher, with her dirty blonde hair pulled back in a ponytail, paces from nervous tension with her eyes fixed on the translucent image of Marcus's sub within the holo display. She is a land warrior and feels out of place in a subaquatic battle. Kris almost lost Marcus before, and she sure as hell doesn't want another scare like that. Her friend Josue watches with her, and he puts a reassuring hand on her shoulder as if to say *Marcus will be fine*.

Back out in the ocean, Marcus and Ray evade heavy fire while desperately searching for a way to disable the hidden depth charges. They zig and zag their subs through the detritus of battle while fighting a path to scan the city for a holo projector that would obscure the mines. The fighter subs have pulse cannons underneath and a vertical row of small torpedoes to each side, but their torpedoes are running out.

Finally, Ray notices a structure similar to what Jon Briar used to project illusory New Baltimore subs into the Battle of New Charlotte. He quickly patches in to the *Virginia*, "Kildare to Gupta. Prapti, are you there?"

"Yes, Ray. What's going on?"

"Your sensors have a much farther range than mine. Scan that structure just off the southwest side of the main bubble dome and tell me if it's letting off a holographic signature."

"I'm on it... yes, it's faint but it's there."

Marcus was listening so he immediately breaks off and races toward the structure, leaving bubbles in his wake. There's a problem, however: the fighter subs have a better chance of sneaking through the network of depth charges, but he could still very well slam into one. So, while curling away from a volley of fire from a gray New Richmond sub, he patches through to the *Myrmidon*, "Taylor to Kim."

"What's up, Marcus?"

"Brendan, I need you to do a calculation for me. Go back to the time index when our subs slammed into the depth charges, note their location and probable trajectory, and let me know the best place to sneak through the web."

Dr. Kim analyzes the data and answers Marcus by sending him the ideal coordinates within seconds.

"Thanks, man. Now I'll feel even worse when I kick your ass in *Sea Strike* after this."

"Since you owe me one I'll actually *try* now instead of just letting you win."

Marcus smiles at this and then moves his small sub full throttle toward the coordinates while saying, "Ray, I'm going after that target – cover me."

Marcus maneuvers through the heavier part of the battle, with enemy subs and drones swarming everywhere. Ray follows him through the water and blasts any enemy ships near him, clearing a path. They both take a few laser blasts but their shields are barely holding. Lieutenant Taylor reaches the spot from Brendan's coordinates, takes a deep breath, and speeds through the wall of depth charges… he makes it past the coordinates safely and exhales, but can't relax because more enemies bear down on him now that's he's made it through. Ray and other Unified subs try to cover him as best they can. A few pulse shots hammer into depth charges, triggering frothing explosions that destroy enemy subs while obscuring Marcus from them.

Marcus corkscrews through the ocean to elude enemy pulse cannons until he's right near the holo projecting bunker. Another feature of these new fighter subs is that they can be armed to turn the entire sub into a moving bomb. Marcus grabs the remote control, pushes the button to arm the sub and eject, and feels his seat moving back into the coffin-like lockout trunk behind him. Marcus enters the tight, claustrophobic lockout trunk; water quickly fills it up and he starts breathing through his gills – a sensation he is much more used to now. Lieutenant Taylor then egresses into the ocean, feeling stunned from the cold of the water, but he quickly gains his bearings and uses the remote control to send his armed fighter sub careening right to the bunker at full speed. Enemy subs get there too late and only manage a glancing shot off the last of the force shield… and then Marcus's former fighter sub *crashes* into the bunker, causing an enormous *explosion* that sends blast wake undulating through the ocean. Marcus does a backwards somersault while subs and drones tumble or sway in the water.

The obscured depth charges suddenly phase into view, and the Unified fleet streams toward the city like Pamplona bulls.

Miranda and her soldiers swim through openings in the depth charge network with the grace of creatures who call the sea home – swiftly going through the water with great swooshes of their flippers until they're knocking right at New Richmond's door, blasting enemies at will. Ray and the other fighter subs slip past the mine grid like flies through a screen door. Once they're through the *Myrmidon* and other attack subs blast depth charges out of their way to surge toward the city through the frothing sea.

Marcus drifts in the water, and sees the *Virginia* swooping toward him. However, a sub drone detects him and turns to attack; it will reach him before Prapti does. Marcus smirks, unslings his pulse rifle, and gets ready to play patty cake with the motherfucker. Luckily the drone already discharged its torpedo, but it starts sending pulse blasts his way. Marcus swims as hard as he can to just barely dodge the blasts before returning shots of his own. He shoots the drone's weapon system, rendering it unable to fire, and then picks it apart with unabashed glee. Just then the *Virginia's* tractor beam ensnares him and pulls him into the lockout trunk on the stern.

Marcus floats in the lockout trunk as water rushes out, cascading over his muscular body, and he thinks, *Damn, I was just starting to have fun!*

The water finishes draining out, and then the door to the lockout trunk opens and Kristin comes in to meet him as he's removing the top of his black combat wet suit. They embrace and embark on a long, deep, passionate kiss. Kristin gets all wet from the water dripping from her man's dark skin, but she doesn't care.

Ahead on the *Virginia's* bridge Dr. Gupta 🜁 gets ready to implement the next phase of the plan. The attack sub battles its way until it's directly facing New Richmond's command hub. Prapti says, "Good luck" to the empty air and pushes a button that makes two holographic tethers lash out through the water and connect with the city's main computer. She then transmits two very special computer programs directly to the enemy command hub.

Jonathan Briar and Kephera gradually phase into solid form in the middle of an empty corridor. The two holographic lovers embrace and give each other a deep, sensual good luck kiss before running off in opposite directions. Jon is heading toward the controls to the city's force shield, while Kephera heads toward the control center for the drones and depth charges.

Kephera turns a corner to find herself confronted by a squad of corporate soldiers. She smirks and waves her hand – attempting to surge holographic energy into their smart chips and knock them out… but it doesn't work. Kephera thinks *oh no* and then phases into noncorporeal form so the laser blasts from the grinning soldiers go through her translucent body. She would not be killed if they hit her with a laser blast in solid form, but her core program would be reset back to its location in the *Virginia's* computer banks – similar to respawning in a video game. Kephera and Jon can't afford to have that happen with either of them. So Kephera somersaults away from the laser blasts, phases to solid form, and then attacks the soldiers using martial arts that Kris taught her. Kephera proved to be the perfect student because she immediately incorporated everything into her program after only one training session, and she is now the equivalent of a multiple degree black belt. Kephera quickly phases in and out of corporeal form to avoid being shot while rocking the soldiers with spinning heel kicks, palm thrusts, and every other move from her extensive arsenal. Kephera flickers in and out while dancing around the room in a furious blur of hand to hand combat.

Jonathan also encounters a room full of soldiers, and when his technique of zapping their smart chips doesn't work he says, "Oh shit…" out loud and phases out while the soldiers converge to send laser blasts through his translucent body. Jon stands there with laser beams shooting through him and says, "Briar to Kephera. Apparently these soldiers do *not* have smart chips."

Kephera's voice comes in, "I see that, and I'm a little busy right now... you should have let Kris teach you how to fight!"

"I know – but what now?"

"You'll just have to improvise, sweetheart. I'm going to use Kris's fighting skills to battle my way to the control center. Kephera out."

Jonathan thinks *fuck*... and decides to just run for it in translucent form. The soldiers follow him, continuing to blast through his apparition-like body, until Jon reaches a door. He can't open the door unless he phases in. Briar quickly looks around the room: on one side there is an elongated window with the ocean and a view of the raging battle on the other side, but the rest of the room serves as a guard station... with several desks and chairs. Perfect.

Jon dives away from the door and behind a desk, quickly phases in, and before they can shoot him he makes holographic energy surge out from the walls to pick up the furniture and send it hurtling toward the enemy soldiers. The desks and chairs knock over a few of them, and Jon phases out again as laser blasts from the remaining soldiers go through him. Jon leaps behind another one of the desks, phases in, and then makes energy from the window's force shield leap over to zap the hands of the upright soldiers, making them drop their weapons while wincing and cursing in pain. Jon then stands up, manipulates holo-energy to pick up furniture while holding his hands out like an orchestra conductor, and then draws his hands back to send the pieces of furniture careening right into the heads of the New Richmond soldiers – knocking them all out. Jonathan breathes a sigh of relief before continuing his journey.

As for Kephera, she fights her way to the drone control center while leaving behind a trail of battered soldiers like bread crumbs in a fairy tale. She flashes into a ball of light and zooms across the ceiling until reaching her target, and when she flutters into the room the few soldiers in there take shots at her while the employees dive for cover under their desks. Kephera morphs back into human form while kicking a guard in the face, knocking him out cold, and then she waves her hands to send holographic energy into the smart chips of the workers, knocking them out as well. However, there is one more guard to take care of, and he looks quite formidable: a huge, muscular man. He shoots his laser pistol at Kephera but she bounds out of the way and makes energy zap from the wall to knock the weapon from his hand. He barely even flinches from the pain, and stands up with a menacing look – daring her to try him, as he stands between Kephera and the control panel.

Kephera has no choice but to fight him. She takes a deep breath and gets into a fighting stance as the large man approaches, grinning confidently. They exchange a few blows that the other parries, feeling each other out, and then she drops down and tries to sweep his legs out from under him. He's too big to topple, though, and he reaches down, grabs Kephera by the throat, lifts her up, and tosses her across the room, making her crash into a row of chairs.

The living hologram simply springs up, with an angry look on her face, and then uses energy from the omnipresent holonet to lift up some chairs and draw them into the man's back, knocking him off balance. Kephera runs up, kicks him in the nuts, and then leaps up, turning to a beam of light for a split second as a furious punch goes through her harmlessly, and then she phases back in and gives the man a sensational flying kick that sends him toppling backwards. Kephera leaps on him and cracks him across the face a few times until he's completely knocked out, and she feels guilty about enjoying it. Kephera gets up, goes over to the main panel controlling the drones and depth charges, and flickers as she suffuses herself into the system – looking like a protean cascade of light and color.

After a few moments she succeeds in shutting down the system. Out in the ocean the depth charges go still, disarmed, while the ominous red eyes of the sub drones go dim as they halt in the water like toys with dead batteries. The Unified fleet can now approach the city practically unabated, with only a few manned subs and divers in their way (divers that are being cut to pieces by Miranda and her aquatic soldiers).

Jonathan rushes toward the command center that controls the force shield over the city's main hangar, and he once again knocks out the guards using a combination of flying debris and energy shooting from the holonet-infused walls and ceiling. He steps over the unconscious bodies of the guards and into a tech room full of frightened employees. Jon says, "Everyone, I know you're scared – but rest assured that I am *not* going to kill you. I simply need to knock you unconscious so that none of you interfere. You may have a bad headache when you wake up, but you'll be okay. Get ready." The employees in the room, with their security badges and formal business clothes, wince in anticipation until Jon shoots energy into their smart chips as gently as he can. The employees slump forward on their desks. Jon quickly goes to the main terminal and suffuses himself into the system. His experience from doing this at the Battle of New Charlotte pays off and he is able to take control of the system within moments, deactivating the force shield and opening the threshold of New Richmond.

Miranda and the others surge toward the rapidly filling lockout hangar with the ferocity of suddenly freed predators. Hapless enemy divers swim in their way in a futile attempt to stop them. Miranda literally slices one of them in half with her machete while making another do a lifeless backflip through the ocean with a pulse rifle shot. Ariel and Margot team up to destroy an attack sub with surgical blasts followed by a well-placed bomb. Shelly slashes an onrushing diver in half and his body parts drift like balloons.

Aquatic soldiers swim into the lockout hangar and wait for the water to rush out, licking their chops in anticipation, with very nervous looking New Richmond soldiers on the other side. By now the news of what Miranda and her unit did at the Battle of New Charlotte has drifted like a rampant wildfire, and these soldiers are *not* looking forward to engaging them. The last of the water drains out and the shield drops, and the aquatic soldiers swarm in to cut their enemies to pieces, committing a level of slaughter that would make Genghis Khan wince.

The M.E.R.M.-Aids dominate the New Richmond soldiers and take over the bubble dome in less than an hour. The city is theirs.

Chapter 2

A large, ornate pleasure sub surfaces in the Atlantic Ocean over Seatopia. The enormous, richly colored ship slowly rises from the sea with water cascading over the hull like sand in an hourglass.

This particular pleasure sub is on a private cruise in celebration of a recent merger between The Peleus Corporation and Thetis Technologies, two of the most powerful corporations in the Seatopia Plutocracy, and this is a highlight of the voyage: a sun party.

Merger guests line up at doors that lead out to the pleasure sub's roof, a deck that is usually submerged with the rest of the ship – but not today. The wealthiest passengers are allowed to be first in line, and once the pleasure sub is completely above water these lucky guests go through the doors and out to a beautiful, sunny day. People emit sighs of pleasure upon feeling the glorious sun on their skin; there are few pleasures greater than this for people who spend most of their lives beneath the sea. Holographic representations of the sun are simply no substitute for the real thing, and passengers slowly make their way out to the deck while soaking up the rejuvenating rays. These parties are such a rare treat because it can be dangerous for a sub to expose itself like this, so armed guards patrol the upper deck on the lookout for enemy missiles and other threats.

The party starts in earnest once most of the guests emerge from the lower decks, with live music, spa treatments, food prepared by some of the finest chefs in Seatopia, and aesthetic sun-themed cocktails circulating around the deck on floating trays. Many party guests simply choose to sun bathe on plush deck chairs, relishing the joy of doing nothing in a state of complete relaxation, while others dance, partake in the entertainment, or stand against the railing enjoying the breeze and looking out over the vastness of the ocean (from above for a change).

Amidst this bliss are two passengers who are not enjoying themselves as much as others. Chad Alexander Fullerton and

Elizabeth Eris Chastain are dead last on the guest list, and they traverse the deck in business suits rather than leisurewear. Mr. Fullerton tries to avoid eye contact with people he used to control, before he was blamed for the takeover of New Charlotte and cast from the corporate council in disgrace. Pharmadyne's stock plummeted after the battle, and the surviving members of the pharmaceutical company's prior leadership now live as pariahs in Seatopia (except for General George Ironwood and his soldiers, who always fight for the highest bidder). Fullerton's wife was only with him for his power and fame so she divorced him shortly after he was let go. Despite the stress and expense Chad sees his divorce as the ordeal's only silver lining because he can now be open about his relationship with Liz – the one person who has been with him through thick and thin. Chad Fullerton and Elizabeth Chastain love each other with abounding passion.

The lovers now live a life of humiliation, constantly belittled by their rivals despite still living in relative luxury, but they have a proverbial wild card that they intend to play on this cruise. Chastain sees one of the three powerful CEOs who she requested a meeting with (Derek Jupiter from Olympus Legal Corporation, the largest and most powerful law firm in Seatopia) and nods at him to convey that it's time for the meeting. Jupiter is a tall man with dark hair and a neatly trimmed beard. He is technically middle aged but you wouldn't know it from his impeccable plastic surgery. Jupiter and one of his muscular bodyguards follow Liz and Chad to an elevator, and the four of them ride down in awkward silence to a corporate meeting facility called The Ida Center.

They step out of the elevator, and the two lovers lead the Olympus Legal CEO to a decorative meeting room. They walk into the room and Jupiter gruffly says, "This better not be a waste of my time" before sitting down at the table and buttoning up his sport coat with his bodyguard standing by. There are a few other bodyguards in the room along with a beautiful young woman holding a briefcase in a business suit, short skirt, and heels with her blonde hair pulled back in a tight bun. Two other CEOs are seated at the table: Dr. Martin Memnon from Memnon Industries and Debra Pallas from Cranium

Corporation. Martin Memnon is a tall, amazingly handsome young man with blonde hair and green eyes. The attractive young woman is his personal assistant, Iris, and his most trusted bodyguard is by his side: a large, muscular Mexican man named Hector. Memnon Industries is a secretive, mysterious corporation and nobody really knows the extent of their endeavors, somewhat like Willy Wonka's chocolate company, but they are mostly known for producing a wide array of holographic entertainment. Debra Pallas is an older woman (who looks younger from plastic surgery of course) with curly, brunette hair. Cranium Corporation has a monopoly on educational wetware and controls all of Seatopia's holonet education.

Liz immediately quells the restlessness of her busy, powerful guests by opening up her purse and taking out the most beautiful, most mesmerizing thing that anyone in the room has ever seen: a golden, spherical object with tiny, polychromatic lights blinking in a random, sporadic pattern. Everyone in the room is transfixed on the object, admiring it with unfailing attention.

Chastain places the beautiful golden sphere in the center of the table and says, "This is the reason why Chad and I asked you to meet with us today. We call it The Eye of Odin, and we will sell it to whoever offers us the fairest deal."

The three CEOs admire the object for a few more seconds until Jupiter breaks the silence, "I must admit it's very beautiful, but please tell me you didn't bring us down here just to auction off a *trinket.*"

Fullerton assures him, "The Eye of Odin is not a trinket, Mr. Jupiter. Scientists loyal to Pharmadyne discovered the object in an ancient chamber beneath the Mariana Trench." The CEOs react to this as such a discovery was mentioned on the news, but with only a few, vague details. Chad continues, "The scientists who analyzed this say that the technology inside is far, *far* beyond anything known to humankind."

Pallas asks, "So where did it come from?"

After a brief pause Liz responds, "The chamber where it was discovered had writing in an incomprehensible language with characters unlike anything ever used by humans." Chastain feels a chill reverberate through her body as she says this. "So the leading theory is that the Eye is of extraterrestrial origin."

This triggers skeptical groans and glances from Pallas and Jupiter, while Memnon just continues to stare at the object without saying a word. Pallas says, "Let me get this straight. You expect us to bid money on something that was supposedly created by *aliens*? What does it even *do*?"

Chad lights up at this question and responds, "Ah, now we're getting somewhere. The real beauty of the Eye is its power. Scientists could study the object for generations before realizing its full potential, but the one thing this device can do for sure is find information… *any* information, anywhere. Within seconds. In fact, through this device we recently learned of the attack on New Richmond before it occurred; we warned them but as we all know those bastards from the so called Unified fleet took over the city anyway."

Liz says, "We gave the object its name because in Norse mythology the god Odin traded one of his eyes for ultimate wisdom, and that's essentially what this thing can give. This device can access any piece information anywhere in the world, regardless of how secure it is, as long as the info existed in some kind of electronic form for at least a few seconds. The Eye also verifies the accuracy of information it finds. It is the most efficient and most powerful information gathering tool ever created."

The CEOs look intrigued, but a skeptical Jupiter looks at both Chad and Liz and says, "Forgive me for being blunt but your track record at Pharmadyne doesn't exactly instill trust. Prove it. Do a demonstration so we know you're not lying."

Liz says, "Very well. You can ask the Eye questions in a few different ways: you can verbally ask it directly, direct the question toward it from your smart chip, or simply formulate the question in your mind."

Pallas says, "Formulate the question in your mind?"

"Yes, the scientists who examined this believe that the Eye has a sort of intelligence, and it can communicate through telepathy. I know that's hard to believe but I can assure you that your skepticism will be short lived. Let's think of a question we can use for a demonstration."

The three CEOs and the two former Pharmadyne leaders have a brief discussion and decide to ask a question about President Barker since he's a public figure they're all familiar with. Liz smirks, looks directly at the Eye, and asks, "Tell us something personal about President Thomas Barker; a potentially embarrassing secret."

The lights on the Eye move in a fluid motion similar to a flock of gulls soaring across a sunset, and within three seconds everyone in the room learns about President Barker's very interesting bathroom routine. Debra Pallas can't help laughing at the ridiculous imagery while Jupiter simply says, "Disgusting" in a gruff tone.

Everyone in the room verifies that they learned the exact same thing about the President (something they don't *want* to know but it's too late), and the CEOs seem impressed.

Liz then tries to drive her point home, "Now why don't you each test it for yourselves. Think of something only *you* know: a deep, dark secret. Don't worry as the Eye will only project the answer to you this time. If the Eye projects the correct answer into your mind, then you will know that Chad and I have been telling the truth."

Everyone around the table takes a deep breath and concentrates on the Eye. Chad and Liz subtly clasp hands and smile at each other because Liz knows and validates his main secret. The Eye transmits a unique image to everyone around the table. After a few seconds Pallas and Jupiter inhale suddenly and look up, astonished. You can practically see the skepticism melting from their faces. Memnon simply grins and nods in understanding: the understanding that The Eye of Odin is indeed legitimate.

Memnon then turns around and nods at his assistant, who turns a knob on her briefcase. All of a sudden the room is filled with a high pitched sound that makes everyone gasp and squirm in discomfort except for Memnon, Iris, and Memnon's two bodyguards (who are wearing discreet ear plugs). The bodyguards take laser pistols from inside their sport coats and blast the bodyguards of the other CEOs, making them crumple with burning holes in their lifeless bodies. Pallas screams upon seeing this, but her screams are quickly silenced when Hector blasts her in the face, turning it into a mass of drooping red gelatin. Derek Jupiter, one of the richest and most powerful men in the world, grips the table tight in helplessness and abject terror. A smiling Memnon reaches into his own sport coat, pulls out a small yet effective laser pistol, and shoots Jupiter right in the chest – making his dead body topple backwards along with his chair.

Dr. Martin Memnon calmly stands up, turns to a stupefied Chad and Liz, and says, "Please forgive the extreme measures but I simply *must* have this thing." Liz starts to reach into her purse but Memnon gesticulates at her with his laser pistol and she thinks better of it.

Fullerton says, "This was supposed to be a peaceful cruise. What do you want with us?"

"We've already established that I will be taking the Eye, but I would also like to offer you both a job with me."

Liz says, "Why would we work for a murdering psychopath?"

"Because if you don't accept my offer then we'll shoot you both right now."

Chad responds, "What kind of an offer is that?"

"One I suggest taking. This 'trinket' of yours is more valuable and more important than even you realize, and we could make a great team using it together."

"I suppose we have no choice."

"Very observant. Now let's get away from this mess before the authorities show up. Know that if you try anything with me at any time then I will kill you both instantly."

Memnon leads Chad and Liz through the door with his pistol pointed at their backs, and he puts the pistol in his coat pocket once they're in the hallway. There is no one around except a few distant caterers, who didn't hear the violence in the soundproofed meeting room. Chad and Liz hear a faint electronic humming from the room and then Iris comes through the door holding her briefcase, followed by Hector and Memnon's other bodyguard. Liz tries to discretely ask what Iris was doing in there and what will happen with the bodies but Memnon whispers, "Shut up…" and pushes the pistol against her back. The party heads toward Memnon's private sub at a nearby docking bay.

They all board the lavish, spherical submarine and the vessel detaches from the pleasure ship to glide away through the water. Once they're underway Memnon motions Chad and Liz over to a display table. Memnon says, "Your first and most important assignment will be to find this woman for me." He powers the table on with a wave of his hand, and the image of a beautiful blonde woman with green eyes hovers above it.

Fullerton reacts in recognition and says, "Wait a minute, I know her: that's Jon Briar's electro whore. What in Ocean's name would you want with *her*?"

"Her name is Kephera, and she is a sentient hologram - something completely unheard of until now. This woman is quite possibly the most precious and most important entity in the entire world."

"I don't understand. She was created for *sex*. What, does she give blowjobs that make you see God or something?"

Memnon just ignores Fullerton's facetious tone, "Kephera can use her consciousness to traverse the holonet at will, and if her powers are honed then she could do even more than that. Think about the possibilities here. Her holographic consciousness could link with the Eye's intelligence to unlock its potential. Any force that combines her abilities with The Eye of Odin would be practically unstoppable."

Chapter 3

Several weeks have passed since the Unified fleet took over New Richmond. Dr. Gupta and others stayed in the city to set up a more inclusive new leadership structure, and Kephera began addressing the city's rampant mental health problems by planning addiction clinics and suicide prevention centers and then overseeing their inception.

With some positive momentum built up and the bubble dome fortified the *Virginia's* crew members are now heading back in good spirits. President Thomas Barker is making a speech about New Richmond over the holonet, talking about how the city could thrive like New Charlotte has since the fall of Pharmadyne.

Brendan, Prapti, Miranda, Marcus, Kris, Ray, and Jon are hanging out on the bridge, with Kephera doing some much needed self-maintenance in the ship's computer system. Miranda left Shelly in command of the *Myrmidon* with the rest of the fleet, and Shelly's new lover Josue is with her as communications officer on the aquatic soldier command sub. Our heroines and heroes are making the secret journey to The Enclave for some much needed down time, and water rushes past the viewport on the bridge while the *Virginia* streams through the ocean.

Ray and Jon (whose holographic body flickers occasionally) talk about the trouble that Jon and Kephera encountered in the assault, and how concerning it is that the soldiers did not have smart chips. This means that the Plutocracy is actively thinking about ways to defend against Jon and Kephera's abilities, so the two electronic lovers will need to evolve their programs to handle such unexpected setbacks in the future.

Brendan and Marcus celebrate the recent victory by playing *Sea Strike 21*, a holo game they both love. Brendan easily defeats most opponents but Marcus is a refreshing challenge, and they each win about half the time. Male friendships tend to be based on mutual interests and competition, so being evenly matched helps strengthen the bond between them. Small holographic attack subs float through the virtual water exchanging volleys of weaponry while the friends use their minds and mellifluous waves of their hands to maneuver their fleets like conductors with two competing orchestras.

Kristin walks up behind them and says, "So how's the bromance going?"

Marcus and Brendan don't respond as if to say *not now, we're concentrating.*

Kris looks over and exchanges a good natured eye roll with Miranda, who is munching on a delightful snack of raw fish. There are few things more boring to them than watching their men play holo games.

The M.E.R.M.-Aid leader says, "Aren't we involved in actual, *real life* submarine battles… *all the time*? So why do you two need to play games about it?"

The two men simultaneously pause the game and slowly turn around to give Miranda the stink eye before turning back and resuming play.

Eventually the last of Dr. Kim's attack craft explodes in the simulated water, they shake hands after a very satisfying game, and a victorious Marcus turns to his girlfriend and says, "Would you like to play, baby?"

"No offense dear but I'd rather use an electric eel as a dildo than play your stupid video game." Miranda laughs so hard at this comment that she spits out one of her fish.

Brendan then says, "Kephera, are you here?" to the thin air.

The beautiful hologram emerges from the wall as a flash of light, slowly phases into solid form, and says, "Sure, Brendan."

He turns to her and says, "Can I talk to you in private for a few minutes?"

Brendan and Kephera go into a private chamber and shut the metal door behind them. Kephera sits down and crosses her legs, and Brendan sits down and sighs before saying, "Even though it's been a few months I'm still not over what happened on the *Rickover*, when

I watched Blake die right in front of me. Someone I cared about. He was my student and we worked closely together for years, but he was also a friend." Kephera just listens intently, and he continues, "When the *Rickover* got hit with the blast I watched Blake's face literally fry off as he died screaming. That image is burned into my mind like a brand; it's the first thing I see when I wake up, and it's the last thing I see before I fall asleep in Miranda's arms. I just can't get it out of my mind and it's driving me nuts."

Kephera says, "It's completely understandable for you to experience that after what you went through. That sub was like a home to you and the crew was like your family, and you watched all of them die. You may be experiencing something called 'survivor guilt', which is fairly normal after a situation like yours."

Brendan nods at this; he looked up the condition and it makes sense because he *has* been feeling guilty about losing his crew, especially Blake.

Kephera brushes hair out of her face with her left hand before asking, "Tell me, Brendan, have you had trouble sleeping since the incident?"

"Yes… yes I have, actually. I especially have trouble sleeping when Miranda is away on a mission."

"Do you think that's because you see her as a bastion of safety, since she rescued you from the sinking sub?"

"That sounds about right, yes."

"You love her very much, don't you."

Brendan smiles and says, "Yes, of course – more than anything."

Kephera smiles at this as well, and then says, "You mentioned that you relive the experience through imagery. How about nightmares? Do you have nightmares about the explosion?"

"Yes… not every night, but maybe a few times a week. Again, they happen more when Miranda isn't around." Brendan looks up at her and says, "So… do you think I have post-traumatic stress disorder?"

Kephera gives him a good natured frown and says, "Brendan, therapists don't like it when patients diagnose themselves."

He smirks and says, "Sorry. So you're my therapist now?"

She says, "Well… it's unethical for a therapist to work with someone they personally know because it clouds objectivity, but I'm technically not a therapist. I'm a friend who is programmed with knowledge of mental health, and as your friend I want to help you. The good news is that PTSD is very treatable. When we get back to The Enclave let's meet in a holo chamber and we'll work on making you feel like *you* again."

Brendan says, "Thanks, Kephera." They hug, and Brendan leaves the private chamber.

Kephera gets ready to phase back into the computer system, but then Marcus enters and says, "Hey, Kephera. I've been meaning to talk to you about something that's been bothering me."

"Sure, what's on your mind?"

Marcus feels the butterflies of impending conflict in his stomach, but he has to get this off his chest so he takes a breath and says, "Kristin told me that you came to her when she was in Jacob Meyer's holo torture chamber. Is that true?"

"Yes, it was the first time I ever saw her. I was exploring the holonet when I encountered a woman in great distress, and I knew she was someone special."

"So… why didn't you rescue her?"

Kephera can tell that Marcus is upset about this, but she explains, "I have very strong instincts, Marcus, and my instinct told me that she would be okay. I *knew* that she would get through the ordeal and that it would end up being empowering for her. Kristin is a stronger, more resilient person now because she defeated that monster."

Marcus, with an angry tone in his voice, says, "Look, Tinkerbell. I've fought in wars, and I've had close friends get tortured to death. It's not some touchy feely enlightenment workshop. So the next time you have a chance to rescue one of us from a *torture chamber*, then you do it. Is that clear?"

"Yes, and I understand that you're upset. Maybe I should have just rescued her, but at the time I wasn't used to *this* world…" she gestures around to the solid matter in the room "…and I have a feeling that Kris might agree with me. She has become my best friend and I care about her too, you know."

Marcus says, "Just do what I said" and then he turns around and walks out of the chamber.

Kephera calls after him, "Sorry, Marcus... but *don't* call me Tinkerbell!" She then turns into a ball of light and floats away.

Chapter 4

Brendan and Kephera walk through a corridor in The Enclave, with water sculptures running through the walls like capillaries in a continuous and ever-shifting flow of color and beauty.

The two friends walk into a holoprojection chamber with circular projectors lining the walls in a symmetric pattern like the pegboard in a game of *Battleship*. They fully enter the room and the doors close behind them. Kephera waves her hand to run a custom program she made for helping Brendan with his post-traumatic stress disorder symptoms, and the room becomes an exact replica of the *Rickover's* bridge. Brendan's beloved ship now lies on the seafloor with the rest of the Battle of New Charlotte's detritus.

Dr. Kim has an immediate, visceral reaction upon being on the bridge again, where he watched people under his command die before his eyes. One sensor technician named Ashley gave him a frightened, pleading look as she slowly drowned – and that's only one of many such images burned into Brendan's memory. Kephera senses Brendan tensing up, and she squeezes his hand in reassurance before saying, "I would like you to sit in your old command chair."

He nods, and tentatively sits in the chair. Brendan attempts to be his usual, scientific self by saying, "I recognize what you're doing, Kephera. You're using exposure therapy. I've read about this and it has a great deal of empirical support."

Kephera gives him a good natured look of annoyance as if to say *turn off your brain for once, Brendan* and then she says out loud, "I would like for you to relax in the chair. Look around and take in the environment here, as if you're actually on the *Rickover.*" She gives him a few seconds to acclimate and then says, "Now close your eyes, take a deep breath, hold it in for a few seconds, and then let it out slowly." He complies, exhaling deeply, and she continues, "Allow your mind to be clear, continue to focus on your breathing, and allow yourself to be as calm as possible."

When he seems fully relaxed Kephera tells Brendan to open his eyes and she starts running the simulation, but not in the exact order that things occurred. She gradually has him feel confident in less distressing situations – the ship being rocked by a laser blast, the force shield being diminished, and small explosions occurring on the bridge – before she has him experience the more traumatizing stimuli.

Kephera runs the next part of the program, and the giant pulse cannon blast from the large war ship rents through the sub's bow, killing Blake instantly right before Brendan again. Kephera stands beside him and continues to keep him as calm as possible with reassuring statements, while Brendan tenses up in his chair in abject terror. The ship starts to sink, water rushes in, and the protective force bubble around Brendan starts shrinking just like it did in real life. The other crew members die one by one, each one a punch to Brendan's heart, but he needs to relive this in order to overcome it and master his fear. Brendan sweats and breathes heavily amidst the chaos around him until the simulation ends with Miranda swimming up to rescue him. Kephera stops the program there, and then she works on helping Brendan to calm down from the experience. He takes deep breaths in his chair, and when he seems calm Kephera resets the program back to the beginning.

The blonde hologram then processes the experience with her friend, "So, Brendan, tell me what that was like for you."

"It was horrible. I know that it's good for me in the long run, but going through that was really hard; watching them die all over again..."

"I know that was hard, but as you know it's *supposed* to be hard."

Brendan nods, and then says, "I feel a little better, a little lighter if that makes sense, but I know I'm not 'cured' yet."

"It makes perfect sense, and you're correct about not being cured yet. Let's meet here once every few days until your symptoms subside, and let me know if your insomnia improves."

Brendan smiles at Kephera and squeezes her hand while saying, "Thank you."

Chapter 5

New Albany lies nestled just off the new east coast in what used to be upstate New York. Memnon Industries resides in a heavily fortified bubble dome adjacent to the city's main dome, built over the ruins of a university called Rensselaer Polytechnic Institute. After a typical, force-shielded lockout hangar the corporation's private bubble is protected by one of the most advanced security barriers in the world: the polychromatic Prism Gate, with each color representing a different (and ever changing) painful death for anyone trying to penetrate it.

A large courtyard lies just past the Prism Gate, with Dr. Martin Memnon's cavernous executive complex on the other side. Dr. Memnon is partial to ancient Greco-Roman architecture so he designed the main section of this complex like a Greek temple with Corinthian columns, statues, gardens, and dancing water fountains. Rather than rising buildings, Memnon Industries is housed in a series of subterranean facilities that extend below the main section down through the ocean floor.

Memnon, Iris, Hector, Chad Fullerton, Liz Chastain, and several of Memnon's top associates are in a small, circular conference room designed to look like a plush, contemporary Greek amphitheater. Iris goes around the room pouring expensive, real wine into people's glasses from a decorative amphora. A three dimensional image of Kephera floats above a central holopad. Memnon initiates, "I desire this woman more than anything, and I want to know how we can acquire her. The Eye was unable to pinpoint her current location because she lives with a group of outlaws who shield themselves from the 'net. Those outlaws may be the key: if we find them, then we find her. So let's discuss her known accomplices." He then looks at Chad and Liz and says, "I know you've had run-ins with these scum before, so please add anything you can think of."

Memnon presses a button on a clicker in his hand and an

image of Marcus pops up, replacing the image of Kephera. "First Lieutenant Marcus Taylor. An engineering genius and brilliant marksman who actually fought for the Plutocracy during the last civil war before fleeing to the land in defiance of the smart chip law. There he joined Dr. Kelvin Gregory's dissident group, and was captured in New Charlotte on a failed rescue mission. Pharmadyne gave him The Operation and sent him to be executed by the sharks, but to this day he is the only person to ever survive such an execution." Fullerton grimaces when Memnon mentions this. "Taylor was rescued by an intelligent shark believed to be created by the rogue scientists who call themselves The Greek Chorus. He played a key role in the recent takeover of New Richmond, and was last detected heading south from there with part of the Unified fleet."

Memnon says, "The next case is rather interesting" and changes the image to show Jonathan Briar.

Fullerton mutters, "That son of a bitch…"

"Mr. Jonathan Briar. By now most of you know the story, and he has become a sort of folk hero among the Plutocracy's enemies. A virtuoso hologram artist who managed to steal a top secret memo right from under his boss's nose…" Fullerton frowns again at the personal gibe "…and then he sent the memo across the holonet, publicizing the infamous Pharmadyne scandal, while also sending the memo to Dr. Gregory's dissidents. He then committed suicide, but before he died he used his considerable skills to create a holographic copy of himself. Briar is also believed to have created Kephera, his lover."

Chad asks, "Briar's copy and this Kephera woman are both living holograms, so why are we more interested in *her*?"

"Because he downloaded electrical activity from his cerebral cortex into his copy, so the alternate is part human. This causes certain limitations, such as how he cannot stray too far from his core program. Kephera has no such limitations. She is a pure hologram and her consciousness can travel anywhere capable of relaying holographic energy, including anywhere in the world the holonet can access. We'll deal with Briar if necessary, but Kephera is much more powerful."

Martin changes the display again to show a gruff looking middle aged man without a left hand. "This is Major Raymond Kildare, known to be friends with both Lieutenant Taylor and Jonathan Briar. He likely told Briar how to contact Gregory's people. Major Kildare lost his left hand in a civil war and made the curious decision to not pay for a new one. What interests me most about him is that he is the only one of these outlaws with a smart chip, but he covers the chip with a buffering material to prevent it from being tracked."

The image changes to show a good looking, muscular Dominican man. "Josue Velerio, a former mixed martial arts cage fighter. He is now one of the Unified force's top soldiers and is an expert with various forms of technology, especially communications."

Hector smirks upon seeing Josue's image and mentions, "He has a bad left ankle."

His boss gets a quizzical look and asks, "How do you know?"

"Because I gave it to him. We used to fight in the same league, and I had a match against him. He was a tough bastard and it was a hard fight but I won by putting him in an ankle lock submission hold. He refused to tap out so I dislocated his ankle and fractured his heel, forcing the referee to stop the fight when the asshole passed out. Velerio needed surgery and ended up retiring because of the injury."

Memnon smiles, "Very interesting. Thank you, Hector." He switches the display one more time, showing a beautiful young woman with dirty blonde hair in a ponytail. "And finally we have Ms. Kristin Thatcher, a renowned assassin and martial arts expert. A very dangerous woman who was apprehended in that failed rescue attempt, but she managed to escape – another failure by the Pharmadyne leadership."

Liz gives Memnon a dirty look at this personal slight, and Fullerton defends himself, "Look, Martin, stop giving me shit about things I had no control over. It wasn't my fault that the bitch escaped."

"I believe I'm your employer now Mr. Fullerton and I'll 'give you shit' about whatever I please. Besides, I mentioned Pharmadyne as a whole and not you personally, so stop being so damn sensitive. Now what can you tell me about this woman?"

Chad chokes back his anger, composes himself, and says, "When Dr. Meyer probed her mind I recognized her father from when I was a kid. Pharmadyne officials were on a land mission when they captured him after a brief skirmish with his raider clan. They took him back to my grandfather, who was CEO at the time, and my grandfather tortured him to death. Before he died Thatcher kept yelling out something about the Mariana Trench in his agonized ravings. At the time the interrogators had no idea what he was talking about, but many years later we discovered the Eye of Odin's chamber."

"So his daughter could definitely play a role in all of this… that reminds me." Memnon changes the display yet again, this time revealing an older woman with wizened features and lines of deep sorrow and weariness etched on her face. "I looked through the logs from when Dr. Meyer probed Kristin's mind, and I came across this woman: Cassandra Thatcher, her mother. She is a member of the Wheeling raider clan and an apparent schizophrenic, but little is known about her other than that. We could use this woman to lure her daughter out of hiding, which would lure Kephera out as well."

Chastain then chimes in, "I still have connections with the Seatopia media. Perhaps we could fabricate a story that would motivate Kristin to pay her mother a visit."

"Excellent idea, Liz. Put those wheels in motion. I want you all to use the Eye and any other tools at our disposal to find and capture both Kephera and Cassandra Thatcher, then bring them to me. Kill the others, and make them suffer if you can."

Chapter 6

Brendan, Miranda, Marcus, Kris, and Ray walk through the farthest, most clandestine part of The Enclave. They all have backpacks full of camping gear (with Jon and Kephera's core programs and a holoprojector in Ray's pack), and they're on their way to a much needed vacation. Everyone except Brendan is very curious about where they're going.

Brendan leads them to what looks like a wall of solid rock, but a beam scans his retina and the wall disappears, revealing a large set of elevator doors. Dr. Kim punches a code into a panel and the doors open. Everyone follows him in, the door closes, and the elevator gently lurches to a start as it begins to rise.

The elevator picks up speed as it rises further, yet the ride feels smooth. The others look at Brendan as if to say *where are we going?* He answers them with the amused smile of a parent quelling an excited child.

The elevator takes a long time to reach the top but eventually lurches to a stop. Brendan punches in another code, and the doors open… revealing bright sunlight that makes everyone squint and shade their eyes until they acclimate. People who live beneath the sea aren't used to such brightness.

They all walk out of the elevator into a halcyon valley of lush grass and flowers, with a light breeze caressing their skin. It's a beautiful day. Birds and butterflies glide through the fresh air, there are mountains in the distance and a crystal clear lake that ripples from the gentle breeze.

In the 22nd century a place like this is beyond precious.

Kristin is the only seasoned land dweller among them, and she is the last to emerge – cautiously. She knows to be skeptical from past experience. The elevator disappears after she exits, hidden by holographic energy. Kris says to Brendan, "Shouldn't we put up a force shield in case of a swarm, and shouldn't we scan for raiders?"

He responds, "This valley is completely surrounded by impenetrable mountains, so there are no swarms and the raider clans can't get to us. The entire valley is force shielded and concealed by a hologram ruse and a sensor dampening grid, so we can't be detected by Seatopia copters and drones either."

"Are you sure this isn't just an advanced holo chamber?"

"I can assure you, Kris, this place is entirely real. We're on the surface right now, in a near perfect location that The Greek Chorus cultivates in the utmost secrecy."

Kristin has literally dreamed about a place like this, so she hugs Brendan before walking through the grass after the others.

When Miranda reaches the lake she phases in her flipper and dips into the fresh water. Marcus sets up his tent while enjoying the demulcent breeze and invigorating sunlight on his flesh.

Ray yells out, "I think it's time to bring out our electronic friends" and he sets up the holoprojector with the two core programs loaded. Ray turns it on and Jon and Kephera phase into the serene meadow by the lake. They initially appear in their formal pleasure sub attire but quickly morph into their active wear after taking in their environment.

The slightly transparent lovers look around in near disbelief as they watch their friends enjoy the beautiful day… and the bright sunlight.

Kephera inhales in awe, looks up at the radiant, life giving orb in the sky, and says, "That must be what humans call 'the sun', although it has many names: Sol; Soleil; Sonne; Guwing; Jua; Taeyang. I have dreamed to see this, Jonathan."

Jon then gets an idea and calls out, "Hey Ray, please put the projector on maximum range."

"You got it, buddy."

Jonathan and Kephera take each other's hands and slowly drift up toward the sun like Icarus and Daedalus, allowing the energy to soak into their faces. They float in the air for a while, taking it all in, before exchanging a playful look. They clasp their hands tighter, and then test out the holoprojector's full range by rising even closer to the sun in an aria of elation. Jon and Kephera then coalesce to become one in a scintillating tumescence of light and color; a mystical fireworks display of affection.

While watching this Ray turns to Marcus and says, "They're really something, aren't they?" and Marcus nods in assent, mesmerized.

Kephera and Jon finally detumesce, become two again, and then gradually drift back to the ground. Kephera, her hands clasped in Jon's, says, "I think I know my last name now."

Jon smiles and says, "What is it?"

"Soleil. My full name is Kephera Helen Soleil."

Brendan puts on scuba gear on the shore of the lake, while Miranda waits for him in the water. They prepare for their swim in an easy, comfortable silence. When they're ready, they exchange the glance of lovers enjoying each other's company with the rest of the world melted away, and submerge into the refreshing lake.

Brendan and Miranda swim beneath the lake with myriad fish drifting all around them while beams of sunlight streak through the fresh water. They swim through a drapery of cascading foliage, and after getting through to a clear, open section of water Brendan takes Miranda's hand and makes a signal indicating where they should swim. Miranda follows him, watching bubbles percolate from his mouth piece, and she sees her lover swim into a rocky, cavernous area and then go up toward the surface. Miranda continues swimming behind him, and they both encounter a circular opening in the rock atop the water.

Brendan and Miranda puncture the surface to be greeted by the sound of a rushing waterfall. Brendan removes his mouth piece and gasps while Miranda reacts as her lungs take over from her gills. They paddle toward each other with only their heads above the water, and then embrace in a deep kiss while letting the waterfall's sound wash over them. The two then pull their bodies out of the water to find themselves in a subterranean cave with a waterfall gushing down on one side and bright sunlight streaming through a small opening on the other. Beneath the beam of sunlight there is a patch of lush grass with butterflies calmly fluttering just below the opening.

Miranda looks at Brendan as if to say *is this place real or am I dreaming?* Her boyfriend answers by simply squeezing her hand and smiling. They sit on the shore while removing some gear. Miranda sits at the edge with her flipper in the water, occasionally splashing with her tail.

Brendan sits next to her and says, "This is my favorite place in the world, and I wanted to share it with you."

"It's amazing; the most beautiful place I've ever seen."

"I knew you'd like it."

"This has been a magical day, and it's great having you explore my world with me."

"That's one of the many things I love about you, Miranda. I love the majestic beauty of the ocean, and the peacefulness of being under water. In a way you're an embodiment of that, and I always feel safe and calm around you."

Miranda gets a somber expression as she thinks about this, and says, "Yes… but I was bred to kill. The ocean can be peaceful, but it's also a world of violence and a constant fight for survival. Most of my life has been about preparing for combat, training for killing the enemy. It's why I was created." Miranda takes Brendan's hands in hers before continuing, "But then I met you, Brendan. You taught me that there is more to life than killing. You taught me about humanity, and love."

Miranda pauses for a moment, and then says, "I have something for you…" She reaches into a pouch on her wetsuit and produces a small, black velvet box. She opens it to reveal a wedding band of solid gold (a ring that Kephera, Kris, and Prapti helped her pick out). Brendan looks at the ring in awe, and Miranda says, "Will you?"

Brendan stutters for a bit, and then his intellect takes over and he says, "Um… you and I definitely have compatible pheromones, and we can't stand being apart."

Miranda gives him a bemused look and says, "Is that your way of saying yes?"

"Sorry… yes, Miranda. *Yes.*"

She smiles, slides the wedding band onto the ring finger of

his left hand, and then leans forward to kiss her new fiancé. The two engaged lovers then lie down on the lush grass, remove each other's clothes, and make passionate love beside the water, listening to the waterfall in the background.

Brendan loves how Miranda's tail flutters when she has an orgasm.

Back at camp Ray embarks on a long hike while Jon and Kephera stay behind in their holoprojector to engender their own reality like artists with a vast, blank canvas. They cherish their private time together in their electronic nation of two, like swifts curling around a waterfall into a secret cave only they can reach. Jon and Kephera have been exploring what it's like to be holograms, pushing the boundaries of what they can do – so in this intimate moment they decide to push the boundaries of their lovemaking.

The essences of Jon and Kephera collide in a dance of mutual arousal, working at each other's epicenters of pleasure. Riding a rollercoaster with no strap, no harness, no seat, and no track – just gliding through midair in an angelic fluid of pure, unadulterated pleasure until they reach an empyrean crescendo that mortal humans could barely dream of. One elongated, soul quenching orgasm subsides just as the next one begins to build until they become one and surf together on wave after wave of ecstasy.

After being lost in time and each other for a small eternity they finally collapse onto their pleasure sub bed in an embrace of exhaustion and contentment.

Meanwhile, Kristin and Marcus just stay in their tent and fuck until their genitals are raw.

Chapter 7

Ray and the others are building a campfire and getting dinner ready when a jubilant Miranda and Brendan pop up from beneath the lake. They get out of the water and start removing their dripping wetsuits, and then Miranda holds up Brendan's left hand to display the ring to everyone. Kris and Kephera (who figured that Miranda would propose) greet the newly engaged couple and fawn over the gold wedding band on Brendan's finger.

A short while later everyone sits around the fire enjoying each other's company as the sun sets behind the mountains. They laugh and talk about many different things, but eventually Miranda reminisces about their success at the Battle of New Richmond, "One thing I love about that battle was how we all came together as a team to win it and get that crucial supply line between the two cities, even though it was harder than we expected." She then turns to Marcus and says, "That was some great swimming out there, worthy of an aquatic soldier. I'm not surprised though because you have an extra propeller between your legs, although it's probably just a tiny little tent fan."

"Yeah right. My propeller could have powered the Titanic around that iceberg and you *know* it."

Everyone laughs at this, including Kris – although part of her is a little wary of the apparent chemistry between her man and this sexy, exotic woman of the sea.

Ray then brings up something serious, "Miranda, you mentioned how we encountered so much resistance, which means New Richmond knew we were coming. Does anyone have a theory about how they knew?"

Brendan ponders the question for a second and says, "Well, in this day and age it's hard to keep anything a secret because sensors are so sophisticated and everything is monitored. It's one of the reasons why this place is such a precious escape. Maybe a Seatopia deep sea station tracked us and warned the city. Which reminds me, I should let you all know that I've been designing a new stealth sub."

Marcus asks, "I've seen you working on it. How is it different from the stealth subs Kelvin used?"

"It's larger and uses more advanced holographic technology so the sub is even harder to detect." He looks at Jon and Kephera and says, "I've been examining the technology that makes you guys work and it's beyond anything I've ever seen. I was able to emulate it somewhat, and the new sub uses similar technology to disappear in the water. It literally becomes invisible."

Marcus says, "Like 'cloaking' on *Star Trek*? What the Klingons and Romulans used?"

Brendan smiles and says, "Yes, that's a perfect analogy."

Kris butts in, "What the fuck is a Klingon? You guys never make sense when you talk about this geek-ass shit."

Miranda says to Marcus, "My foot is going to cling on your *ass*, motherfucker." Miranda and Kris laugh at this, and Kephera can't help laughing too.

Marcus just ignores them and says, "Damn, that would be *very* useful."

The conversation reaches a lull, as most conversations do. It's completely dark now, and everyone sits in relaxing silence listening to the crackle of the fire, the sound of peepers, and the playful splash of a frog leaping into the lake.

Jon hasn't spoken much tonight; the flesh and blood Jon was always shy, and his new holographic self remains that way because he programmed his personality to be as similar as possible. He breaks the silence by looking at Brendan and saying, "I agree that this place is a precious escape. The old me really needed a getaway like this; it could have helped his depression. Does this place have a name?"

Brendan smiles at his hologram friend and says, "We decided to not give this place a name because… it just somehow didn't seem right. It just *is*. But if we need to refer to it we simply call it 'The Sacred Place.'"

Everyone chats for a short while longer and then turns in to bed. Jon and Kephera kiss goodnight and then dematerialize into their holoprojector, Kris and Marcus go into their tent and zip it up, Ray goes into his tent, and then Brendan drags his sleeping bag to the edge of the lake so he can sleep with his future wife, whose legs phase back into her natural flipper as she slips into the water. One obstacle the lovers face in their relationship is how Miranda prefers to sleep in water and can't spend an entire night with her legs phased in, so if they want to sleep together then Brendan has to sleep at the edge of a pool. Tonight Miranda snuggles into his arms with her flipper dipping in the lake, and they drift off to a peaceful sleep enveloped by the gentle sound of water caressing the shore.

The next morning a bleary Kristin stumbles from her tent and starts making coffee. Kephera phases in to soak up the morning sunlight. She notices bags under Kristin's eyes and says, "Did you have trouble sleeping?"

Kris looks at her and says, "Marcus snored like a banshee on a kamikaze run." Kristin then faintly hears a beeping noise coming from her backpack, and gives Kephera a concerned look. She told their friends back at base to only contact them in an emergency.

Kris pulls the secure comm from her backpack, says, "It's Josue" and then answers.

"Kris, are you there?"

"Yeah, what's going on?"

"We intercepted a broadcast from several Seatopia networks. Apparently something terrible happened to the Wheeling Clan."

Kris inhales in shock. That was the clan she grew up in – her family.

Josue continues, "According to the report Seatopia recon drones detected a massive explosion at the clan's most recent camp, and many were killed or injured. Also… the report said that the clan's shaman was badly wounded. Isn't that your mother?"

Kris tries not to panic, "They could be full of shit, Josue. This is the Seatopia news network we're talking about here."

"You could be right, of course, but the story was broadcast on many different networks, including one that's known to be legitimate.

The level of agreement indicates that the story may be true."

Kris tries to fight back tears as she says, "Okay, Josue. Thanks. We'll be back as soon as we can. Thatcher out."

Chapter 8

Kris and the others cut their vacation short and are now back at The Enclave, in the same meeting room where Brendan and Marcus spoke with Secretary Bryson about mobilizing the M.E.R.M.-Aid unit.

Josue shows Kris the broadcasts in question, and then Kris turns to her friends and says, "We have to go after her. I *have* to see if my mother is okay, and if she's not then we need to help her."

Brendan says, "Going to the land is very dangerous – you know that better than any of us. Going all that way to find one woman is just too risky, and whoever goes out there will be vulnerable. We're at war, Kris; we've won a few battles but we're still vastly outnumbered and need to stay hidden."

"I know it's not the logical or rational thing to do, but she's the only blood relative I have left." Kris then looks around at her friends, who have become like a surrogate family, and says, "My dad died when I was a kid, and if my mom dies without me even trying to help her then I will never forgive myself. It would haunt me forever. If you don't help me go after my mother then I'll just go on my own, and you won't be able to stop me."

Marcus steps up, hugs her, and says, "You know I'll be with you no matter what, so count me in."

The others (except Brendan) follow suit, and everyone agrees to accompany Kris on the search for her mother. Dr. Kim finally gives in and says, "Well… I guess it's time for the maiden voyage of the *Surcease*."

Brendan leads his friends and a group of Unified soldiers to a docking bay in a lower level of The Enclave. They all turn a corner and see Brendan's big new stealth sub. The *Surcease* is oval shaped and looks like a sleek turtle shell, with faint green lights around the perimeter, torpedo tubes where some of the plate markings would be, a main viewport on the front, and an advanced tractor beam and lockout trunk on the back. There's also a cargo hold in the belly with a few small fighter subs and a hovercraft for land transport.

Everyone walks down into the sub and inside it looks similar to other Unified subs, with a command bridge and pools for aquatic soldiers or intelligent sharks like Hendrix and his friends. One difference is that Brendan made this sub as aesthetic as possible, and inside there are panels with soft coagulations of light designed by Jonathan; the various colors slowly undulate like a 20th century lava lamp. Brendan and Jon thought that having artwork on the ship would help people remain calm in heated situations.

Josue will be serving as communications officer and Marcus will work at tactical so they both sit at their stations. Josue's girlfriend Shelly will be staying behind with the *Myrmidon* to command the aquatic soldiers while Miranda is away.

Marcus turns to Brendan in his command chair and says, "So I'm curious about where this sub's name came from."

"I called this vessel the *Surcease* because that's what I feel when I go under the waves. I love the ocean, and when I go under water in a submarine I always feel a sense of surcease; a halt to the craziness in the world above – especially now that I'm not as bothered by what happened to the *Rickover*." Brendan looks over at Kephera as he says this and she smiles back at him. "Perhaps the only good thing about what's happened to humanity is how we're now communing with the ocean like never before. So let's experience the namesake of this ship." Brendan gives the command to start up the engine and set out on their voyage to find Cassandra Thatcher.

The *Surcease* backs away from the docking tube and turns away from The Enclave. The scientists' hideout shimmers in the water and disappears, replaced by the appearance of an underwater cliff, and then Brendan's new sub starts picking up speed – heading north, toward the part of the land closest to the Wheeling Clan's last known whereabouts.

A few minutes later Brendan says, "Okay, everyone – it's time to go invisible. Prepare to cloak."

The lights inside the sub dim and the hum of technology

fades. The *Surcease* shimmers and gradually disappears in the ocean, with only a patch of open water where it used to be.

The journey is uneventful for the first few hours; the omnipresent waiting game in a life of combat. Most of the crew never tire of watching water stream by on the viewport as the *Surcease* races through the ocean, and the meaning of their new sub's name sinks in at a primal level as they experience the serene, austere beauty. Josue then sees a light blinking on his station as a proximity detector starts beeping. He brings up a four dimensional map of the area and sees a cluster of gray, cylindrical Seatopia patrol subs near them in the Atlantic.

He turns to Brendan and says, "Dr. Kim, you'd better take a look at this."

Brendan looks at the holomap and smiles, "This is exactly why I built this sub. Just stay on course, we'll be fine."

In the past they would have had to fight their way out of a situation like this, but the patrols are unable to detect the invisible *Surcease* so they glide right by the enemy subs – practically across their bows. The Seatopia subs don't notice them at all, despite having their sensors on maximum, and the Unified crew continues on their journey.

The crew of the *Surcease* approach their destination just off the new east coast, northwest of New Richmond near the border of what was West Virginia. The water gets shallower and they drift over houses and rusted cars that are now habitats for sea life. Kris looks down from a viewport and shudders when she sees fish swimming through a barnacle-encrusted swing set on an old playground. They get close to shore, and now the question is how to track down Cassandra's current whereabouts.

Kephera says, "Brendan, I assume that this sub has holonet access."

"Of course, although we use a buffer to prevent being tracked, kind of like Ray's smart chip protector."

"Then I'm going to travel into the holonet. I'll be back soon."

Kephera phases into light and suffuses herself into the nearest terminal.

Several seconds later she phases back in and gives the coordinates for Cassandra Thatcher's most probable location.

Brendan, Ray, Josue, and Marcus all give each other stupefied looks and Marcus says, "How the hell did you do that?"

"It was easy. I simply searched the holonet with my consciousness, bypassed Seatopia's security codes, and examined the logs for their recon drones. The most recent log had the coordinates for the Wheeling Clan that I just gave you."

A very curious Josue asks, "How did you bypass their security codes within seconds? Hacking at that level would take me days, or even weeks."

Kephera laughs, "I don't know how I do it, I just *do* it. For me, bypassing a security code on the holonet is like Albert Einstein doing a first grade math problem. It's second nature."

They all look at each other again, with their jaws practically on their shoes, and Marcus says, "Kephera, why didn't you tell us about this before?"

She crosses her arms and says, "It just never came up."

Brendan then steps in, "Do you know what this means? You're probably the most efficient and most effective spy who has ever lived!"

She glitters as a plume of light then rematerializes and says, "Thanks. I try."

Jon teases his girlfriend by saying, "Showoff…" after Kephera's trick.

Miranda cuts in and says, "You'd better mobilize for traversing land. I need to stay here and watch over the sub with Brendan because I can't be away from water for that long. Good luck."

Everyone then scurries to their duties, but before he leaves Marcus walks up to Kephera and says, "Hey, I'm sorry I snapped at you earlier."

"It's okay, you had a point – but I stand by my argument that it was empowering for Kris. Friends can agree to disagree."

Marcus puts his hand on Kephera's shoulder and then goes

off to gather his gear.

The *Surcease* de-cloaks and then rises out of the water like a whale getting air. The extraction team consists of Kris, Marcus, Ray, Josue, several Unified soldiers, and a few holdovers from Gregory's dissident group including Jaclyn and Trenita. Jon and Kephera are phased out with their core programs in a protective case tucked away in Ray's pack. The party boards an armed hovercraft, and the hovercraft drifts from the deck of the sub over to land across the surf. Kris turns around and watches the *Surcease* disappear again as it sinks beneath the waves. She then turns back in wariness as they travel across the ominous land she used to call home.

In the executive complex of Memnon Industries, Hector knocks and enters Dr. Martin Memnon's office to find his boss chatting with Iris. "Sir, the Eye of Odin just told me that Kephera was engaging in holonet activity."

Memnon turns to him and says, "And?" with an interested and impatient look.

"… and she examined the logs of Seatopia recon drones over West Virginia. For some reason the Eye didn't say where she linked in from, however."

"That's strange, but our plan seems to be working. Keep monitoring the situation and let me know if anything new comes up."

"Yes, sir."

Chapter 9

People started fighting over dwindling resources and dwindling land when water levels initially rose in the mid 21st century. Citizens had to leave the engulfed coastal cities but had few places to go. People in neighboring cities were reluctant to help one another, partially due to years of built up animosity over professional sports rivalries. Then the first modern civil war broke out and the United States of America became the United Corporations of America.

Conflict among Americans was exacerbated when it came time to inhabit the newly constructed Seatopia domes. Corporations own the bubble domes and the new corporate government gave higher ranking corporate employees first priority. Wealthy citizens emigrating to Seatopia were allowed to bring a few personal servants at their discretion, which filled up the domes even further.

The Plutocracy then implemented the controversial "seven figure cutoff", which stated that a family would be allowed into Seatopia if their combined household income was at least seven figures. They allowed in laborers with skills necessary for the upkeep and daily operation of Seatopia, and then the domes were closed to any more inhabitants.

A large group of angry land dwellers bum rushed one of the last ships to Seatopia in protest of the seven figure rule. Guard drones rose up and opened fire on the mob, killing every last one of them in what became the worst domestic massacre in American history.

The people left behind on land became more and more tribal and insular until local communities started forming raider clans that battled each other for resources and territory. Most of the land fell into anarchy. There are still some gated pockets of civilization like Denver and Santa Fe, but the people there still live in constant fear like all land dwellers.

Kristin Thatcher thinks about this as her hovercraft zooms

across the scarred landscape. She sees the picked apart ruins of a once thriving society, and looks at crumbling buildings like the ones her raider clan use to take refuge in.

A horrible smell greets the Unified hovercraft and everyone wrinkles their noses in disgust as they come upon a huge landfill. The new east coast is peppered with landfills where corporate drones dump Seatopia's trash and waste. Marcus is driving the hovercraft and he maneuvers it around the landfill when a boxcar-like Seatopia refuse drone flies in from the ocean to dump its load of trash. The drone ignores everyone as it goes about its business – likely because it can't detect any smart chips (and Kephera would use her powers to block any transmissions if the drone did detect them). Everyone breathes a sigh of relief when the drone spins in the air and flies back toward the ocean.

They continue on through a town that seems empty at first, but the people are just hiding from the armed craft passing by. The hovercraft passes a burned out shopping plaza with the dirty faces of curious children peering at them from abandoned shop windows. Kris smiles at a little girl who reminds her of herself, but the child scurries away from the window. The people here are more of a danger to each other; they would have to be crazy or desperate to attack a group of armed soldiers with advanced technology.

A while later they reach the West Virginia wilderness. Some of them feel relieved to be among trees while others find the woods disquieting. Marcus navigates the craft between mountains and around trees as efficiently as he can until his friends decide to take a break to eat and relieve their bladders.

Ray takes a moment to wipe sweat from his brow with his sleeve. It's *hot* out here on land. He starts eating a food ration when he hears Kephera's program beeping in his pack. She's trying to communicate with him. He takes out his comm device and opens it up. A miniature, translucent version of Kephera protrudes from the comm and says, "Ray, I'm scanning the area and I noticed something disturbing. A large cluster of organic matter is approaching your position. Fast."

Ray calls Kristin over and tells her what Kephera said, and

Kris goes pale. She says one word that every land dweller dreads, "Swarm…"

Kris springs into action, "*Swarm*! Everyone crowd in near me – *fast!*"

Marcus, Ray, Josue, and the others follow her orders by huddling as close as possible right next to the hovercraft. Kris takes an emergency force shield transmitter from her pack and starts setting it up.

Marcus hears the most unnerving sound he's ever heard coming from one of the mountains. A chittering. And it's getting *loud*.

A few tense seconds pass.

Then a huge mass of aggressive looking insects curls around the mountain heading straight for them at a lightning pace. It looks like something escaping from the gates of Hell. Marcus can't help screaming – along with everyone else.

Kristin turns the force shield on and it activates in a blink of energy *just* before the wall of raging insects slams into them. The insects chitter against the force shield, with the first wave getting zapped and dying against the electronic wall in a cascade of horror. But they just keep coming like water from a busted pipe.

One of the Unified soldiers was off in the woods taking a piss, and he runs toward the force shield. Amidst the loud chittering Marcus yells out, "Can we let him in?"

A stoic Kris says, "If we let down the shield then we *all* die. We need to let him go. Try not to look."

Part of the swarm converges on the man and chitters against his screaming, flailing body – completely engulfing him. His eyes explode in two small bursts of blood, and the insects strip his flesh like peeling wallpaper, right down to the bone. His blood curdling screams pierce everyone's ears until they die down, which is somehow worse. Trenita drops to her knees and wretches on the ground from watching her friend die. The Unified team eventually can't see him anymore because the shield gets covered.

The insects have red eyes that actually look *angry*, and they ram against the shield like crazed Black Friday shoppers before a store opens. Kris remembers this all too well from her life on land, and she hugs Marcus close to her while waiting it out. Everyone huddles together in a terrified bundle while the bugs keep trying to get at them. To feast.

After several minutes the swarm trickles away from the shield to fly off in search of easier prey, until they're all gone – leaving behind a pile of dead insects around the force shield like fallen leaves from a tree. Kris takes a deep breath, turns off the shield, and everyone looks over at the dead soldier. There's nothing but a pristine skeleton lying on the ground.

Kris says, "Picked clean" before going off into the woods to take the piss she was holding in.

.

Chapter 10

The *Surcease* lies just below the surface near the rendezvous point, invisible. Brendan and Miranda enjoy their privacy despite worrying about their friends, and it's romantic having the sub all to themselves.

Dr. Kim tells Miranda to close her eyes. He then takes her hand and leads her into his private workshop. She hears him remove a sheet from over a large object, and then he tells her to open her eyes while he says, "It's your engagement present, Miranda."

She sees an unusual human bed. It's the size and shape of a regular king sized bed but the surface isn't firm, and it makes a sloshing sound when Miranda presses her fingers into it. There's water beneath the top layer! One side of the bed has a body-sized slit like the opening of a change purse, giving access to the water, while the other side is sealed; there's also a cushioned, comfortable looking barrier in the middle of the bed between the wet side and dry side.

Miranda says, "Um… what is it?"

"It's a custom made waterbed, just for you and I."

"What in Ocean's name is a waterbed?"

"The modern waterbed was invented in 1968 by Charles Prior Hall. They were quite popular in the 1970s and 80s, with their popularity peaking in 1987, but then they fell out of favor in the 1990s."

"How come?"

"Well… I guess they became lame and uncool."

Miranda laughs and says, in a facetious tone, "*You* like something that's old, lame, and uncool – I'm shocked."

Brendan smiles and says, "I know, I know. Anyway, sleeping together comfortably has been a problem for us, and when we were sleeping at the edge of the lake in The Sacred Place I got the idea to build this bed for us. You can sleep in the water while I sleep on the dry part. The middle is designed to soak up excess water so I stay dry, and look…" he pulls out a pair of pajamas with wetsuit-like material "…I made a few pairs of waterproof pajamas for me. So do you like it?"

She leans in, kisses him, and says, "I love it. Thank you, Brendan. You're so sweet."

They decide to christen their new custom waterbed so they embrace and topple onto it together. Miranda giggles at the sloshing sound as they tumble around making out and stripping off each other's clothes.

After they finish making love Brendan gets out something else for his new fiancé: an engagement ring for her to complement the one she gave him. This prompts her to shove him back onto the bed so they can make love all over again.

Back on land the hovercraft traverses the West Virginia hills in a search pattern around the Wheeling Clan's last known coordinates. Everyone is vigilant about another swarm after what happened, but Kephera can't detect any.

Kris eventually sees a slight pillar of smoke on the horizon, points, and says, "There. Marcus, head toward that smoke."

"You got it, baby." He pushes the throttle forward and speeds in that direction, weaving through trees and around rocks, until Kris taps on his shoulder – telling him to cut the engine. She doesn't want to make any assumptions out here so they need to be cautious. The hovercraft glides to a halt near a large clearing and Kris, Marcus, and Josue go up ahead to check out the source of the smoke.

They creep up to the forest's edge, and Kris peers through the trees. It's a makeshift village full of tents, with people scurrying about doing various tasks. Kris immediately sees people she recognizes, and can't help feeling tears well up in her eyes. She turns to Marcus and says, "I'm home."

Kris emerges from the woods and walks with caution toward a group of friends she used to spar with: a thirty-something man with a beard named Kevin, a middle aged bearded man with darker skin named Deandre (who has a rash from a Pharmadyne-created ailment), and a twenty-something, raven haired White woman named Jessica. Three people who were like family to Kris before she joined the dissident group. They all wear the tattered, dirty clothes of people who live their lives in tents, constantly on the run from rival clans, swarms, Seatopia drones, and countless other threats.

Kris walks closer. They hear her and turn with their weapons drawn, but then lower them upon recognizing her. Deandre says, "Kris Thatcher…" and then hugs her tight. Jessica and Kevin hug her in turn, and then Kris waves for Marcus and the others to come over.

Kris introduces Marcus, Josue, Ray, and the rest of them to the members of her old raider clan, who give her a warm welcome back. Kris is a legend here who saved people's lives on countless occasions.

Kristin finally looks over at the shaman hut, the source of smoke, and sees her mother come out through a decorative curtain wearing a lengthy dashiki dress and sandals. Cassandra Thatcher appears to be in her sixties with wispy gray hair and wizened features, but she looks older than she actually is because her stressful life has taken a toll on her. She has blue eyes with the wild look of madness shining from them.

Cassandra walks toward Kris with her hands outstretched and her palms facing upward. Kris walks up to her, clasps her hands, and then they hug with tears welling up in their eyes.

Cassandra says, "I've missed you."

After a brief time Kris releases the hug, looks her mother in the eyes, and says, "Mom, are you okay? We came out here because we heard that something happened to you guys."

Cassandra gives her daughter a confused look at this, and Kris gets a chill down her back while giving Marcus a concerned glance and biting her lip. Marcus feels the concern from his girlfriend and immediately gets vigilant, watching for anything suspicious.

In the meantime, Ray and Josue set up the holoprojector and reassure the villagers as they do so. Ray says, "What you're about to see might shock you, but it's okay. These people are friends." Ray then turns on the projector and the ghost-like bodies of Jon and Kephera start phasing in amidst the villagers' surprised gasps. Jon and

Kephera stand there, and when Cassandra sees Kephera she inhales quickly with her wild eyes going wide, squeezes her daughter's hands in affection, and then makes a mindful beeline toward Kephera.

Cassandra walks right up to Kephera and holds out her hands. Kephera takes the cue by clasping Cassandra's hands and then Cassandra, looking Kephera right in the eyes, says, "Kephera Soleil. I've waited so long for you. *So* long."

Kris and Jon exchange a puzzled glance as if to say *how does she know Kephera's name? And her* last *name at that?*

Cassandra takes Kephera's hand like a parent leading a child across a street, and she walks the beautiful hologram woman back to her hut. Ray sees this and makes sure the projector's range is bumped up to maximum. Cassandra leads Kephera into her hut, and they talk in there for a long time with smoke wisping from a hole in the roof.

During the interim a very nervous Marcus paces around until he turns to Kris and says, "We have to get out of here. There is nothing wrong with your mother, and nothing bad has happened to this clan recently. Those news stories were clearly fabricated."

"I know… but we have to wait for my mother to talk with Kephera. It seems important."

"What's important is not getting captured again, or killed. Why would the Plutocracy make up a story about your mother's raider clan?"

"I don't know. We'll get out of here as soon as we can."

Jon says, with pensiveness in his voice, "I had the chance to kill Chad Fullerton and I let him go. Maybe it was a mistake to let him live; his mistress has a lot of power in the Seatopia media."

Kris says, "It *was* a mistake, Jon. When you have a chance to kill a mortal enemy then you take it. You and Kephera are going to get us killed with your bleeding heart antics."

Jon gives her an assertive look as if to say *back off* and says, "I did what I thought was right at the time. I was keeping my side of the street clean, hoping that Fullerton and Chastain would learn something from my mercy."

Kris sighs and says, "People like them *never* change. This

is a wicked world, Jon. Who knows if Chastain was behind that fabricated news story; it could be anything."

Marcus butts in and says, "So what do we do now? I say we go in there, get Kephera, kiss your mom goodbye, and get the *fuck* out of here."

Kris says, "We can't do that. We have no choice but to wait." She then walks off to catch up with her old friends.

An hour goes by. Kris calms her nerves by practicing Qigong, which she uses to relax and cope with her anger. Right now she's waving her open palms back and forth through the air in a gentle, rhythmic sweeping motion, performing a technique known as "waving hands like clouds".

All of a sudden Kephera emerges from the hut with a contemplative expression on her face. Everyone watches as she walks over to Kris, who stops doing her Qigong technique with a smooth motion back to a basic stance.

Kris turns to her friend and says, "So did you understand anything my mother said? She's crazy and it can be hard to tell what she's talking about."

"Kris, there is absolutely nothing wrong with the dopamine levels in your mother's brain."

"So… what does that mean?"

"It means that your mother does not have schizophrenia, at least not in the conventional sense."

Kris gives Kephera a puzzled look. She always just assumed that her mother was a schizophrenic.

Kephera takes a deep breath, reaches out, and holds Kristin's hands tight while looking her directly in the eyes. "Kristin, listen to me. Your mother is a time traveler."

Chapter 11

After a brief pause so this can sink in Kris looks back at Kephera and says, "What are you talking about? This is a really bad time for jokes, Kephera."

"I am absolutely, one hundred percent serious. Your mother is from the future, and she acts the way she does because of time travel psychosis."

Kris gives her friend a look of disbelief, and then sits down on a rock to contemplate the magnitude of this news. She looks up at Kephera and says, "What the *fuck*? What am I supposed to do with this? This makes me completely rethink my entire life."

Just then everyone hears an explosion over the next ridge. Kevin runs up and yells out, "We're under attack! A rival clan is coming at us from over the ridge."

The entire camp starts mobilizing for combat. Kris gets her pack and weapons from the hovercraft and then runs toward the fighting, but her mother flags her down when she passes her hut and says, "I have to tell you some things before you go. In my dreams I see wings of golden light soaring through the heavens. These dreams *must* become a reality, Kris. This is our last chance."

A frantic Kris says, "Mom, *what are you talking about*?!"

Cassandra grabs her daughter's shoulders and says, "We *must* make sure the golden ones survive. I'm serious, Kristin. Please listen to me. Nobody ever does, but this time I *need* you to."

Kris calms down a little and says, "Okay, mom." She makes a mental note to ask Kephera what this stuff means and then asks, "Mom, are you from the future?"

"Yes. Now you need to get out there and help. You've always been our best warrior."

Kris hugs her and says, "I'll kick their asses and be right back. Love you, mom."

As Kris runs off Cassandra calls after her, "The pilot fish that goes backwards can be very dangerous. Be careful."

Kris looks back one more time, shakes her head in confusion, and runs up the hill to see her clan and her Unified friends exchanging fire with onrushing raiders. Marcus and Josue pick off enemies at will from behind a rock. Kris takes cover behind a gnarled tree and joins in the festivities by blasting a hole through a man's body. Jon and Kephera can't help in this battle because there's no holo technology here so they're phased into their core programs in protective cases back at camp.

The Unified soldiers and Wheeling villagers hold off the invaders for a while, exchanging volleys of fire. Several people on either side are shot and killed, and Kris has to watch as beloved people she grew up with go down screaming with laser holes burned in their bodies – but that's just part of life on land.

Ray is standing on a ledge behind some rocks slicing down enemies with precise shots when a raider sends a floating disc bomb beneath the ledge, blowing up the ground beneath him. Ray is stunned from the blast, and he slips on the scree beneath his feet and tumbles down the hill until he bashes his forehead on a rock. He grimaces in pain and reaches up to his aching head... and notices that his smart chip protector is smashed and damaged.

Out at Memnon Industries the Eye of Odin comes to life and a wash of lights swish across the gold sphere. Hector was waiting for the Eye to give some answers, and he gets one. He is still not used to the object *talking* to his mind, but he shrugs off the odd sensation and runs to find his boss.

Hector rushes into Memnon's office and says, "The Eye just detected Raymond Kildare's smart chip."

A cruel smile splays across Memnon's handsome face and he says, "Excellent. Send the coordinates to Fullerton and tell his strike team to head there. Immediately."

"Will do, sir."

Back on land, Marcus sees Ray's fall and has Josue cover him while he runs down to check on his friend. Ray is a little bloody but he's alright; the real problem is his busted smart chip protector, and he conveys that to Marcus with an ominous look. Marcus sees the damage and takes down a charging raider before working on the protective covering. Ray says he has a spare in his pack so Marcus tosses away the smashed one and quickly works on installing the replacement. Every second is a second that the chip could be detected by Seatopia sensors. Marcus finally puts the covering over Ray's smart chip, and they return to battle.

Kris eventually helps her people route the enemy raiders and they watch as the would-be pillagers run off over the ridge and out of sight. There's always a next time though in the endless conflict over food, water, medicine, weapons, and everything else. Kris turns around and leads everyone back, when they hear an ominous whirring sound coming from the far side of the village.

Marcus says, "Now what?"

They all witness Seatopia battle copters soaring into the valley, sweeping down toward the village. Marcus says, "Oh, fuck..." and they all run.

By the time they reach the village copters are spraying the area with laser blasts, killing people at will. Jaclyn runs up screaming and tries to take one of the copters down with her rifle, but the copter simply turns and cuts her to shreds with its laser cannons. Marcus can only stand there watching as the body of his close friend is blasted into chunks of seared meat. He screams out, "No!" and then runs for cover with Kris while trying to hold back tears. Josue runs for an anti-aircraft turret.

There are three large copters strafing the village with fire, slaughtering Kristin's raider clan like cattle. Seatopia soldiers in gray uniforms drop down from one of the copters and run through the village, killing anyone who gets in their way. Kris, Marcus, and Ray reach cover and take out as many enemy soldiers as they can, but they're outgunned and can only do so much.

One Seatopia soldier makes his way to the containers with Jon and Kephera's core programs. Kris thinks *no* and tries to run over and stop him, but her way gets sprayed with laser fire and she has to retreat back to cover. She's pinned down and helpless. A few Unified soldiers stayed back to guard the programs but they get blown to bits by copter fire, and the searching soldier smiles as he reaches the container with Kephera's core program. He cracks the lock's code with a device Memnon gave him and then he opens the container like a pirate finding a chest of doubloons. Kris thinks *how the fuck did he open the lock that easily?* She tries to blast him but he's out of range. Kris lost her father as a child, her entire village is being destroyed all around her, and now her best friend is about to be stolen, or even killed. And there's nothing she can do.

Jonathan then phases out of his container and appears by the soldier with a furious look on his face. Jon gets ready to zap the man's smart chip and knock him unconscious, but a sniper from one of copters blasts Jon with his laser rifle – making him disappear, reset back to his core program. The man smiles at this and takes out a cylindrical, tube-like piece of technology called a holosiphon, designed for capturing a hologram like a firefly in a jar. He places the device against Kephera's core program and siphons her essence into the tube. Kris feels like the man might as well be pulling out her guts. The energy that is Kephera Soleil gets sucked into the tube and ends up trapped in there. The ball of light scurries around the tube in a panic and thumps against the glass to no avail. Kephera knows that something's wrong. The soldier then secures the container, but not before Cassandra Thatcher hits him in the head with a rock, knocking his helmet off. Kris and Marcus can clearly see that the man has a wild haircut like a puffed up blowfish; he also has gills indicating that he's had The Operation. Cassandra runs up to him with a long knife and says, "Leave her alone…" while thrusting with the blade. The man easily parries the stab attempt and is about to kill her but recognizes her from the briefing, so he knocks the old woman unconscious with a backhand blow. The soldier scoops her up and runs off to a waiting copter with Cassandra Thatcher slung over his right shoulder and Kephera tucked under his left arm.

Kris yells out, "Mom… no!" as she watches both her mother and her best friend being kidnapped. The man runs to the copter, and Kris recognizes Chad Fullerton and Elizabeth Chastain there waiting for him. She bristles in anger and hatred.

By now Josue has fought his way to the anti-aircraft weapon and he uses it to fire a small missile right into one of the other copters. It slams into the chassis, crippling the shielding, and then Josue sends a second missile plowing into the copter – making it explode in midair and crash to the ground in a great plume of flame. It's an empty triumph, though, as he can't destroy the copter with Kristin's mother on it. He has to let it just rise up and take off.

Inside the copter Chad Fullerton yells to the pilot, "Let's get out of here. We got what we came for."

The pilot says, "But sir, Dr. Memnon ordered us to kill everyone."

"Fuck Memnon, he's not in the middle of a battle. I didn't know they had anti-aircraft missiles and I don't want to be next. Get us out of here."

"Aye aye."

Before the copter flies away, Elizabeth Chastain looks out right at Kristin, blows her a mocking kiss, and then tosses a holopad to the charred ground. The hovercopter then turns around and speeds off over the mountain with a whirring sound. The other surviving copter flies right behind it.

Kris drops to her knees, lets her rifle fall from her hands, and starts sobbing. Everyone she cares about gets taken away. The man she loves, who survived an execution to come back to her, reaches his arms around her. They hug and Kris cries onto his shoulder, with chaos all around them.

The battle isn't quite over, however. A few Seatopia soldiers were left behind and they're now being surrounded and killed by the angry villagers. An angry Kevin walks up to a soldier being held up by a few villagers and slits his throat, and he's about to kill another one. Kris wipes her tears away and yells out, "Stop! Keep him alive!"

Kevin hears this, nods at her, and sheaths his knife – but clubs the man in the back of the leg with his rifle, dropping him to his knees. Marcus goes over and helps everyone bind the man for questioning, and Marcus notices that the man has gills just like the one who took Kephera.

Kris just sits and continues to cry as she takes in the destruction all around her. She can't help feeling responsible for the destruction of her home, her family. After she composes herself as much as she can she goes over to collect the holopad Liz Chastain tossed from the copter. Kris finds it and makes sure it's not a bomb in disguise. She then picks it up with quivering hands and a feeling of dread in her gut, and looks at it. The pad's screen has an old fashioned, two dimensional note on it that says:

Dearest Kristin,

You may be interested to know that Chad Fullerton's grandfather captured your dad and tortured him to death.

If you seek revenge for this, and we know damn well that you will, then you will beg for death at the end just like your pathetic father.

Hugs and kisses,
Elizabeth Chastain

Kris looks at the note in shock, feeling bile rise up from her stomach as her tears turn from sorrow to anger.

Marcus comes over to her and says, "What is it?" Kris hands him the pad with tears of anger trickling down her cheeks and a frightening look on her face. Marcus reads it over and then gives his girlfriend a look of both disbelief and empathy. He knows his woman, and he knows how this note has stirred up deep-seated, primal rage in her.

Kris shoves Marcus aside and heads over to interrogate the prisoner. He might be their only clue to finding her mom and

Kephera.

The soldier is on his knees with his wrists bound behind his back. Kris storms up to him, pulls her knife out, grabs his hair, and places the sharp tip of the knife right on his throat while saying, "If you want to live then you'll tell us where your people took them."

The man laughs and says, "I have no reason to tell you anything. As soon as they find out I'm still alive they'll send a pulse to my chip and fry my brain. I'm gonna be dead within minutes."

"Well then I'll have to jump right to the fun part. Have you ever had a knife jabbed into your balls?"

"I've heard what you did to Dr. Meyer, you scum bitch. You're gonna get yours."

Kris says, "I'm sure" and then starts slicing open the man's pants.

Jon then phases in, looking upset. He's sick with himself for failing to save Kephera, for letting himself get shot in corporeal form.

Kris points at Jon and says, "Get him out of here!" She then turns to him and says, "I don't want to talk to you. You could have killed Chad Fullerton with a flick of your wrist, but you let him live – and now look at what you've done!"

Jon raises his open palms in a gesture of peace and says, "Kris, I'm on your side. I admit it was a mistake to let Fullerton go, but we don't have much time. Kephera and I have been working on how to probe a person's mind; let me try on him – it's our only chance."

Kris says, "Fine…" with an angry tone and then steps aside.

Jon goes over to the man and starts crackling energy from his hands into his brain like a plasma ball.

The soldier says, "Get the fuck off me."

Jon says, "Shut up" and keeps working. Images float into Jon's mind. The man resists, but he's not very strong minded so Jon pushes the resistance aside. He sees a city of pleasure for people who've had The Operation, and knows that this man used to hunt with Jacob Meyer. He's thinking about an upcoming event in this city.

All of a sudden the man screams and starts convulsing. Jon screams too from a surge of violent energy going through him, and he pulls his hands away while the soldier's brain fries right in front of everyone. The Seatopia soldier slumps down with foam on his lips, dead.

Kris looks at Jon and says, "Well?"

Jon takes a second to recover from being zapped and then says, "I couldn't find out where they took Kephera and your mom..." Kris scowls at this "...*but* I did find out something interesting. As you can see this man has had The Operation, and many corporate soldiers with gills are meeting at a big underwater party that Jacob Meyer used to throw every year. They're continuing the tradition in his honor."

"That motherfucker is haunting me from the grave. Where will it be?"

"At the Reef hotel and casino. Atlantic City."

Chapter 12

Marcus digs a hole to bury the remains of his friend Jaclyn, and feels warm tears trickle down his face as he puts the mutilated body parts into the shallow grave. Everyone in the village is stricken with grief. A sullen Kris talks with Kevin, Deandre, and Jessica about what to do next. She offers to have them come with her and join the Unified force, but they all turn it down as Kris expects. They need to help the village recover from this tragedy, and Jessica was training with Cassandra to become the next shaman. She's now thrust into that role. Kris feels beyond guilty about bringing this destruction on her family, but they love her and don't blame her for it.

The Wheeling people start packing up to relocate yet again in their nomadic life. Hopefully they can find a spot near fresh water, although they'd likely need to fight for such a coveted place and they're in no shape for more combat right now.

Kristin hugs her friends goodbye (holding back tears as she knows she'll likely never see them again) and then gets onto the hovercraft for the journey back to the *Surcease*. Marcus fires up the engine and they glide off to the east through mountains and woods.

The journey back has a few close calls with drones but nothing too bad, and they eventually reach Brendan and Miranda at the rendezvous point. Brendan and Miranda are somber about everything that happened on land and do their best to support their grieving friends. The reality of what has happened sinks in once they're all back down in the inviting belly of the aesthetic new sub: they went to rescue Kristin's mother, but they're coming back without her *and* without Kephera. The mission was a disaster, and now instead of building on their progress at New Charlotte and New Richmond they have no choice but to follow up on their only clue.

The *Surcease's* crew set a course for Atlantic City.

The stealth sub cloaks and the lights go dim as it spins in the water to head for the sunken ruins of New Jersey. Kris is emotionally numb so she just stands at a viewport staring out at the open water. She sees a shoal of sardines swirling in the distance, and stares at it until it's out of sight. Not even the beauty of the ocean can make her feel better right now.

Jon notices her standing alone. He hates conflict but this new version of himself knows the importance of resolving issues before they worsen, so he walks up to Kris and says, "Hey."

"Hey." She keeps looking out the viewport.

"Kris, I feel terrible about what happened. Back in New Charlotte I thought that letting Fullerton live was the right thing to do. I figured he would learn a lesson from my mercy, but apparently he didn't. I've never killed anyone before."

She says, "Except yourself."

Jon is taken aback by her bluntness and after a few seconds he replies, "...well, I guess that's right."

Kris turns to look at her friend, "You're too idealistic, Jon. You need to remember that we're *at war*. When you're at war you need to think about things differently, and you sometimes have to do dirty work that would shock most civilians."

"But I'm not a soldier like you, Kris."

"If you're fighting with us on this sub then you're a soldier whether you like it or not, and you'd better start acting like one."

At this point Ray walks up to listen in.

Jon replies, "Like I said before, I admit that letting Fullerton go was a mistake, but arguing about it won't help. You're probably right about the soldier thing; you trained Kephera to fight and I saw how it paid off in New Richmond." Mentioning his lover's name makes him feel a pang of heartache and he says, "...I miss her so damn much."

"I miss her too, Jon. I'm sorry I snapped at you." Kris and Jon give each other a brief, casual hug before Kris continues, "I can't believe how stupid I was to fall into that trap."

Ray cuts in, "I've been listening to you two beat yourselves up, but I take full responsibility for losing Kephera and your mother because my smart chip alerted them to our location. One thing I've learned from combat though is that you can't look back. Bad shit happens, and when it does you need to do the best you can to fix it. Let's meet with the others to make a plan for Atlantic City."

Chapter 13

Kephera is in human form floating in mid-air with her wrists and ankles in glowing green shackles and a matching collar around her throat, surrounded by a force shielded cell and trapped in a shaft of light that's like hologram flypaper. Her binds become tighter the harder she struggles, so she decides to relax and think about how to escape. She's in an ornate chamber of ancient Greco-Roman décor beneath the executive complex at Memnon Industries, although she doesn't know exactly where she is because her abilities are blocked.

The tall, blond, handsome CEO himself enters the chamber with Iris and Hector right behind. Hector is holding a rectangular metal box. Kephera scowls at her captor, but Memnon ignores it and turns on his politician-like charm, "Welcome, Kephera. I apologize for keeping you like this but we have no choice; you're too important and we don't want you escaping into the 'net. My name is Dr. Martin Memnon. This is my assistant Iris and my bodyguard Hector. You're our guest and we want you to be as comfortable as possible, so just ask and we can provide you with anything you'd like."

"I would *like* to be let go so I can get back to my friends. They were being attacked when you kidnapped me and I want to know if they're okay."

"I'm afraid that letting you go is the one wish we cannot grant, Kephera. I understand that you're upset about being taken against your will, but please know that we have your best interests in mind."

"How is keeping me as a prisoner in my best interests? Let me go."

"Because we brought you here to help you unlock your potential. Your *full* potential."

"I can do that with my boyfriend. He and I have been expanding our abilities together, and you're just some creep who kidnapped me. Let me *go*."

"Kephera, here we know how to hone your abilities to make you the most powerful entity in the world. Rather than a clumsy exploration with your part human boyfriend, here we can show you what a pure hologram can do. Which is practically anything."

Kephera admits to herself that she's a little curious about this, "My friends recently told me that I'm the most efficient and most effective spy who ever lived. I would not act as a spy for a kidnapper like you, but I *am* curious about what else I'm capable of."

"You should be. The abilities you've explored so far are like the tip of an enormous iceberg, and with this device..." Hector opens the box to reveal The Eye of Odin "...you can utilize anything and everything beneath the water. You would be unstoppable."

Kephera gasps upon seeing the Eye, and stares at it like an Australian watching the Melbourne Cup. Transfixed. The object is beautiful, and seems familiar to her... but she can't quite place how or why.

"We call this 'The Eye of Odin'. It's an electronic mystery, just like you. If you learn to commune with it you would be like a key inserted into a lock that opens endless possibilities. You could have power beyond the limits of human imagination, and we can harness that for you."

"I'm not interested in power or riches or anything like that. I want my *friends*."

"I'm not talking about *that* kind of power. The power of money or petty governments. I'm talking about the power of *possibility*, Kephera. Power over reality itself."

Kephera thinks about this and then says, "If you have such good intentions then why did you take me by force? Why didn't you contact me and talk about this in a peaceful way? You could have worked together with my friends."

"Because your friends don't understand your potential like I do, and they don't know about the Eye. If I did what you suggest they would have never agreed to this. Think about the big picture, Kephera. We're talking about unlocking the door to a new kind of existence, a higher state of reality. I brought you here so you can realize the full extent of your powers, instead of squandering them with a ragtag group of vagabonds in a hopeless revolution. Work with the Eye, and I promise you won't regret it."

"Those 'ragtag vagabonds' are the people I love, and I'm not doing anything without them – especially Jonathan. He's a hologram too, so why didn't you bring him here?"

"I told you before that he's part human, which limits his abilities."

"Having a human side is not a weakness, if someone cultivates the good parts of humanity like passion, togetherness, and creativity. Jon has all of those qualities, and his human side is why I love him so much. Anyway, I don't know anything about you, *mister* Memnon. Who are you?"

Memnon bristles inside at the subtle slight. He hates being called "mister" instead of "doctor". He doesn't reveal his annoyance however when he replies, "I am the world's leading expert on holographic technology. A genius, some say. I am the perfect person to help you commune with The Eye of Odin. I'll give you some time to think about all of this."

"Will you release these shackles and let me roam free in here?"

"I'm afraid I can't do that. You're too precious, and I can't risk having you escape."

"Then I've made my decision. I don't trust you, and I will not work with you."

"Kephera, you just got here. Allow the magnitude of what we've talked about to sink in."

"I have. You have taken the things I value above all else: my freedom, my autonomy, my individuality. There is nothing worse to me than being in chains."

"Well… I'm surprised to hear that, because I know how you're turned on by bondage."

Kephera gasps in shock and says, "How did you know that? That's private!"

"The Eye of Odin told me. The Eye can find out almost anything about anybody, and if it's combined with your abilities then you can direct its energy to magnify its power."

"Ewww. Did you actually think you could convince me to use that thing by violating my biggest secret? You really know how to build a woman's trust, Mr. Memnon. Besides, bondage in fantasy and bondage in real life are completely different, and the flesh and blood Jon Briar *programmed* me to like it."

Memnon is smart enough to know that he had her on a hook and was reeling her in, but lost her. The tone in her voice says that there's no going back, and he has to resort to more aggressive measures. His countenance changes and becomes grim, almost frightening, and he says, "I'll ask you one more time. Will you join us and work with the Eye?"

"You know my answer. I have nothing more to say to you." Kephera then breaks eye contact with him and looks away in defiance.

He knew what her answer would be but needed closure before what he's about to put her through. It's a pity; if she cooperated things would be much easier, and she's *so* beautiful.

Memnon sighs and says, "Then you leave me no choice." He nods at Iris, who flicks a switch on her briefcase. Kephera slowly floats to the ground, with the shackles still on her wrists and ankles. Memnon pulls a black, rectangular controller from his belt and pushes a button that makes a thin green strand of energy reach out and attach to the green, glowing slave collar on Kephera's throat.

She says, "Leave me alone…" while struggling against him as much as she can (which isn't much).

Dr. Memnon leads her like a pet on a leash over to a clear, rectangular box in the corner that looks somewhat like an old gas lantern.

Kephera looks at it and asks, "What is this?" with concern in her voice.

"I simply call this 'Hologram Hell'. I predict that you'll be completely insane, and completely broken, within a matter of days in there. Then you'll be my pretty electronic puppet and I'll combine your powers with the Eye whether you like it or not."

Kephera just glares at him with abject, utter hatred.

Memnon nods at Iris, who flicks a switch on the wall. A green beam of energy shoots from the device and engulfs Kephera, then starts morphing her into her true form like an artist molding clay. Kephera shrinks down into a ball of light and gets siphoned into the box. The ball of light ends up stuck in the box's dead center, and tries to break free but can only wiggle slightly. Red laser beams then sear into her from all angles and the consciousness of Kephera Soleil is sucked into Hologram Hell.

Kephera finds herself ensnared in Laocoön tendrils and thrust into a carnivalesque Fellini nightmare rushing past in wild pastels, beset by dysphoric images from the lizard brain of an insane surrealist: a mother watching an angry mob tear her baby to pieces and then devour the bloody limbs; a battlefield ankle deep in blood with attackers scaling a portcullis only to have boiling oil dumped on them, melting flesh from their bones like dripping wax as they emit throat-wrenching screams of death; an artist smashing his easel to bits in a drunken rage and then throwing his life's work onto a bonfire with tears streaming down his face; a fever-crazed horde trying to escape a quarantined city, clawing at the gates and clubbing each other to bloody pulps with anything they can find as mangled corpses pile up; a man clenching his teeth on a stick while a doctor saws off his leg without anesthetic; an accident scene with a little boy watching his mother loaded onto a medivac copter, knowing he'll never see her alive again.

This Ludovico parade of torment culminates in a scene with Kephera's beloved friends swimming in desperation amongst the sunken ruins of an antediluvian city, with sharks circling them… and then *striking* – tearing at their flesh and rending them limb from limb. Kephera's consciousness has to look on as her loved ones are ripped apart over several agonizing minutes until Jonathan is the only one left alive. Sharks chew his body from the bottom up until they reach his heart and wrench it from his torso, with screams bubbling from his mouth as he dies in agony and his face goes still. The sharks devour the remaining dead meat until there's nothing left but a huge cloud of blood in the water. All of this amidst the forlorn, anguished wails of filthy inmates in a barbaric asylum.

And then the pain. Memnon tries to reprogram the essence

of Kephera Soleil with malevolent spikes of energy that stab right to her core, and twist.

Screaming.

Screaming.

Chapter 14

Miranda stands behind Brendan's command chair, looking out the *Surcease's* main viewport with the lights dimmed from the sub running invisible. The deep ocean water gets shallower as they approach what used to be the New Jersey coast.

Miranda points and says, "There…" as she sees a barnacle-encrusted Ferris wheel on the rotten, collapsed boardwalk that is now a marine life habitat. A few sunken boats dot the seabed around the city. The small dome's lights appear and she can see beautiful casinos within, with several parts of the city extending free out into the water. This new version of Atlantic City is unlike anything Miranda has ever seen: a haven for water breathers like herself.

Atlantic City went through a rough patch in the 21st century when the casinos faced competition from legalized gambling in many other places. The once thriving gaming and entertainment mecca was abandoned when ocean levels rose, but when The Operation came about a group of entrepreneurs decided to turn the sunken city into an underwater playground for those who've had the procedure (people known as "aquas"). The city is a hybrid with dry sections and other sections that are completely underwater – chambers designed as an homage to the ocean's splendor.

As the only water breathers on the *Surcease* Miranda and Marcus will have to infiltrate the city, pretend to be guests at the aquaparty Jon saw in the soldier's mind, and find out where Kephera and Cassandra are. Miranda feels some rare nervousness about this mission; she can handle straight on fighting just fine, but she's not used to espionage.

Jon needs to work his magic before his two friends can leave for their mission, however. Brendan hides the *Surcease* behind the remains of an old fashioned "wild mouse" rollercoaster, and undoes the cloak for just a split second so he can send an energy tether through the water. Brendan transmits Jonathan's core program along the tether and Jon suffuses his consciousness into the city's computer. Jonathan surges through the network and finds information about the Jacob Meyer memorial aquaparty in the underwater section of the majestic Reef hotel and casino. Jonathan adds two more names to the guest list, with pictures of the holodisguises that Marcus and Miranda will use. Jon successfully completes his mission without being noticed, and extricates his consciousness back to the *Surcease*. Jon tried to find the whereabouts of his girlfriend in the city's computer network but not even he could reach such highly classified information; he knows the irony that Kephera is the only one who could do that.

So now it's up to Marcus and Miranda. They take a shuttle to Reef's lockout hangar in the guise of hotel guests with invitations to the aquaparty. A tractor beam pulls them in, and they park their sub shuttle in the hangar just like regular hotel guests. They pass the kiosk where you can get buffet coupons by signing up for a slot chip, and they follow the rest of the hotel guests into the lobby (which is dry as some guests are not water breathers). Marcus and Miranda walk into the cavernous lobby and are stunned by its beauty. The entire room looks like a coral reef of myriad colors, with marine life swimming around in aquariums designed to look like they're part of the lobby itself rather than in separate enclosures. The disguised "couple" stops to look at a display with various jellyfish pulsating and undulating in their arpeggiated dances of being.

Marcus and Miranda check in and go to their room. Nobody seems to be following them, and nothing seems out of the ordinary. Their room continues the coral reef theme, with the bed designed like a comfortable, inviting oyster shell. Hopefully they'll find out what they need before having to spend the night here. They have the option of keeping the room dry or filling it with water, and they keep it dry for now. The two water breathing members of the *Surcease* crew start getting changed for the aquaparty: Miranda puts on a black, waterproof evening gown that goes to her waist and will blend in with her flipper later to make a natural-looking ensemble. Marcus puts on a waterproof tuxedo – a suave black and white tux made with wetsuit-like material. He looks in the mirror and straightens his black bow tie. They put comm shells in their ears and miniature snorkels in their mouths so they can communicate under water; aquas can choose to have a private conversation with one other person by directing a comm beam at them (somewhat like tagging someone in the ancient game known as "laser tag") or they can widen the comm beam to have a conversation with multiple people at once.

Marcus then gives Miranda a facetious smirk as he extends his elbow in a chivalrous gesture. Miranda returns the smirk, slips her arm through his, and they head off to their mission.

The holodisguised Unified soldiers get to the dry foyer outside the party at a wing of the hotel that extends into the water outside the main bubble dome. They stand in line as guests are checked in, trying to hide their nervousness and hoping that Jon's trick worked. Bouncers check Miranda and Marcus in without incident, and wave them into a transition chamber. The two friends stand with a group of other party guests somewhat like people being loaded onto a theme park ride. They can see into the party through the thick, clear panel, and it's one of the most beautiful places either of them has ever seen: the main room is like an elaborate nightclub except it's under water and full of coral reef displays and wisping mangrove trees with marine life swimming amidst the party guests. Seahorses float by with their tails clasped in affection; a giant potato cod sits on the sandy floor like he owns the place; sea turtles swim right past party guests who laugh with bubbles coming out of their mouths as they imbibe alcohol in little tubes attached to their mini snorkels; and countless colorful reef fish swim about everywhere.

The transition chamber starts filling up with water and Miranda phases in her flipper. This brings about startled glances from a few other party guests, but they don't say anything because rogue aquatic soldiers are spotted at Reef every now and then – and a few are on the guest list tonight. Miranda fumes upon thinking about these rogues as the water level continues to rise. There is nothing that Miranda hates more than a deserter, and after The Battle of New Charlotte a few victorious aquatic soldiers decided to abandon the M.E.R.M.-Aid unit for a cushy life in Seatopia. Such women are in great demand because of their strength and exquisite beauty, and it kills her inside but Miranda is masquerading as one of those deserters tonight.

Marcus and Miranda feel the water overtake their heads, and Miranda feels at home. This is *her* world. They swim into the party, and it's like being inside an aquarium designed by an artistic genius. Cirque performers swim through protean hoops in an impressive array of underwater acrobatics. In a coral-enclosed corner there is an aquaband with a star soul conch player; a band member weaves a measured, billowing bouquet of polychromatic bubbles while their trance-inducing dub music pulsates through the water to permeate people's entire bodies. Aquaparty music is meant to be felt more than heard.

Lieutenant Taylor and Lieutenant Colonel Ulmo decide to blend in by swimming right over to the "bar" (a horizontal rushing current with aqua bartenders behind it who hand out tubes filled with whatever alcohol the patron requests). Marcus and Miranda order and pay for their drinks, and as they're waiting Miranda looks across the room and feels a rush of anger upon seeing the rogue aquatic soldier she hates more than any other: Sergeant Wendy Wrasse, a ringleader who convinced others to desert with her. The spitfire with short, dark, curly hair worn in the style of a 1920's flapper is enjoying the attention of several wealthy-looking men in watertuxes. Lieutenant Colonel Ulmo manages to contain her anger and stay focused on the mission. She decides to ignore Wendy and keep her distance so she doesn't lose her temper.

They get their drinks, insert the tubes into their mini snorkels, and split up to search for anyone who might be connected with the Wheeling Clan attack. Marcus wades past a giant clam and it snaps shut, startling him.

Miranda and Marcus swim around with their eyes peeled, trying to be discrete. They explore the party for about half an hour, until Marcus sees something from the corner of his eye: spiky hair that looks like a puffed up blowfish. It hits him - that's the same guy who abducted Kephera and Cassandra. Perfect.

Marcus sees Miranda elude some potential suitors by

swimming through a hole in a coral wall. He swims over and gives her a serious look that says *I've found something.*

She looks around to make sure nobody is watching and cocks her head toward an alcove by a tunnel that leads to the darker, more discrete area of the party with bioluminescent fish. They swim into the alcove, Marcus directs his comm signal right at her, and says, "I just saw the soldier who kidnapped Kephera and Kris's mom."

"Are you sure?"

"Yes. I could never forget that haircut." Marcus describes him and then says, "What should we do?"

Miranda smirks and says, "I'll go over and seduce him, then I'll lead him up to our room. You follow us, and we'll interrogate him when we get to the room."

Marcus can't help smirking back at her plan. This might be fun. "Sounds good, I'll hang back while you charm him with your siren song."

Miranda subtly gives him the middle finger in a playful way and then swims over toward their target. She swims around a school of clown fish and when she reaches the spiky haired man he's treading water and talking to Wendy Wrasse. Just great. Miranda swims around his vicinity, trying to ignore the men attempting to hit on her, and when there's a lull in the conversation Miranda swims across from the man and gives him *fuck me* eyes. That should get his attention. He kisses Wendy's hand and says goodbye to her for now, and decides to chat with this mysterious new aquatic soldier. He introduces himself as Dash. Miranda and Dash talk for a bit before wading over to a recess in the coral wall to flirt.

Marcus treads water over by a four dimensional, underwater version of roulette (in which a ball spins around in a bubble chamber and ends up in one of many black or red tubes) and discretely watches their exchange.

Miranda and Dash eventually clasp hands and swim into the labyrinthine network of bioluminescent caverns. Marcus swims behind them, but keeps his distance. The dim underwater caves are for party guests who want more privacy, and there's an unspoken rule to avoid any alcove occupied by a couple. Miranda grabs his hand and leads him through the caves full of glowing fish until they find an unoccupied alcove. Miranda pulls him in, removes her mouthpiece while also removing his, and kisses him with bubbles emanating from her mouth. She feels icky about making out with an evil bastard who abducted her friend, but it's all part of the job. She starts running her hands all over his body, and rubs her right hand against his crotch – feeling him harden under his watertux pants. He returns the favor by feeling up her breasts, and after they make out for a while Miranda puts her mouthpiece back on and suggests that they go back to her room. Dash can't believe his good fortune; there is no woman more desirable than an aquatic soldier, and he will have prime bragging rights among the soldiers in his unit if he has sex with her.

The two of them swim out of the dim caves and back through the main party room to the exit. Miranda's flipper phases back to legs, and Dash sees that she's wearing black fishnets under her dress. He is so horny that he can barely think. They go back out to the dry part of the hotel, towel off, and then head up to Miranda's hotel room. Marcus tails them from a distance.

Miranda leads Dash to her room, opens the door, and brings him in by the hand. She kisses him and starts undoing his bowtie, and his penis is harder than a diamond. All of a sudden Miranda spins him around and cups her right hand over his mouth so he can't scream. Marcus hears this from out in the hall so he comes inside and shuts the door. Marcus and Miranda turn off their holodisguises and Dash's eyes go wide as he recognizes the black man from the strike team's briefing: the boyfriend of Cassandra Thatcher's daughter. Miranda continues cupping his mouth with her right hand, slips her left hand over the man's throat, then says, "You know how strong aquatic soldiers are, so I'm sure you know I can snap your neck with a flick of my wrist. Now tell us where you took Cassandra Thatcher and Kephera. I'm going to lift my hand from your mouth, and if you scream you die." She cautiously removes her hand from his mouth while Marcus points a laser pistol at him.

He struggles to get his breath and then says, "We were hired by Memnon Industries near New Albany, and that's where we took them after leaving the village. That's all I know."

Miranda says, "Thanks, motherfucker" and then reaches out to grab his neck.

Marcus sees what she's doing and says, "Miranda – no!" but he says it too late...

Miranda *snaps* the man's neck, and his dead body crumples to the floor. She turns to Marcus and says, "What? We found out what we needed to know."

A panicking Marcus says, "Miranda... an off duty soldier's smart chip is programmed to send out a signal if they die." Just then a klaxon on the hotel floor goes off, triggered by the dead man's smart chip. Marcus gives her a dirty look.

"Oh fuck..."

"Oh fuck is right. Run!"

Miranda grabs a laser pistol and they run out into the hallway. Perturbed hotel patrons come out of their rooms wondering what the noise is about, and a group of Seatopia soldiers run toward Marcus and Miranda from their end of the hall – blasting at them with pistols. Hotel patrons dive to the floor or flee back into their rooms in terror. The *Surcease* crew members return fire, taking down two of them, then turn around to run in the opposite direction. Marcus and Miranda race toward a stairway, but the door opens and a few more Seatopia soldiers emerge. Marcus and Miranda fire at them but they're outnumbered. One of the soldiers sends a remote control flying disc whirring down the hall toward them, and it sprays them with knockout gas. Marcus and Miranda start coughing, drop their guns, and collapse onto the lush carpet of the hotel hallway.

Darkness.

Marcus wakes up on a cot in a detention cell, and feels very groggy. Drugged. Miranda is curled up in his arms with her flipper phased in, and she moans upon waking. So sleepy. She nuzzles against him, and they take solace in the warmth and security of each other's presence. Murky thoughts pass through Marcus's mind. They're lucky to be alive at all, and now they're prisoners in a city filled with Seatopia soldiers – who could show up any minute now and drag them to a torture chamber.

They're likely about to die a slow, painful death, and Miranda feels so good in his arms. God she is so beautiful. There has always been sexual tension between them. But she's Brendan's girl, and he loves Kris. Miranda nuzzles against him again, sighing with grogginess. Their faces nestle together, with their lips close. The primal part of yourself comes out when faced with death, and they can't help exchanging a kiss. The one kiss becomes another, and another. It feels good so they hold each kiss a little longer, until they embrace and explore each other's mouths in deeper, passionate kisses. Marcus curls his legs around her flipper and their making out gets more rigorous, with heavy breathing. Marcus can't help fondling the aquatic soldier's near perfect breasts while Miranda runs her hands all over him and brushes against his gills. They kiss and fondle for a while in a drugged daze of passion, until Miranda looks down her arm and sees the glimmer of her engagement ring.

She gasps and pulls herself away. This knocks Marcus into awareness too and he feels guilty about Kris. They sit with the awkwardness, waking up and coming to their senses, and after a glance that says *we should forget about what just happened* they turn their attention to the task at hand: getting out of this cell. They *must* tell the others where Kephera is.

The groggy warriors take in their environment. They're on a lone cot in a small cell surrounded by a force field. The cell is in a larger room with a guard sitting at a terminal by the door. He's looking at porn on a holopad, not paying attention to them.

Marcus turns to Miranda and whispers, "So how can we take down this force field? Any ideas?"

Miranda bites her lip, thinking, and whispers back, "You know… there is a chip inside my lower back that controls the phasing of my legs. It uses technology similar to a force field."

Marcus smiles and says, "Perfect."

He goes to reach behind her and feel for the chip, but before he does Miranda puts her palms against his muscular chest and says, "That chip is in a very intimate spot."

"Would you rather wait here until they interrogate us?"

"Just be gentle."

Marcus nods in understanding and rolls Miranda onto her stomach as quietly as he can. He feels around until he notices the chip, and then starts working on it.

Marcus spends a few minutes tinkering with the chip. With one step left Marcus leans forward behind Miranda's left ear and whispers, "I got it. As soon as I take down the force field we need to silence that guard. Get ready."

Miranda phases her flipper into legs.

Marcus takes down the shield, and they race into action. The guard is still occupied by his porn but notices the prisoners rushing toward him so he tries to slap the alarm. Miranda springs with lightning quickness to catch his wrist and break it while Marcus knocks the man out with a clubbing blow. He turns to Miranda and says, "He only has one gun."

"I don't need one."

Marcus pulls the laser pistol from the man's holster. They bind him and gag him and then go into the hall with caution. There are two guards in the hallway. Marcus blasts one and Miranda subdues the other with a backhand strike. She picks the man up, his face a fountain of blood after just a light blow from her, and says, "Which way to the ocean?" The man points and she knocks him out with an elbow strike and takes his pistol. Marcus and Miranda run for it in that direction. They appear to be in the bowels of the hotel, an area devoted to security and maintenance.

The two escaped prisoners turn a corner to find a squad of Seatopia guards in an ornate ballroom. Miranda glimpses her aquatic home through a large viewport beyond the room before shooting the closest soldier. She then tucks the pistol into her fishnets and somersaults across the floor. Miranda springs up, grabs two soldiers, breaks their necks, and then uses their bodies as human shields – with one in each hand. Enemy fire piffs into the dead bodies as Miranda approaches the guards like a bulldozer. Marcus uses the bodies as cover too while he picks off Seatopia soldiers at will. Reinforcements start arriving and the fighting heats up.

They battle their way close to the viewport, which looks out at the sunken boardwalk and Ferris wheel, leaving a trail of littered bodies in their wake. Miranda drops the two mangled corpse shields and they take cover by leaping over a bar right in front of the viewport. Laser blasts shatter the liquor bottles atop the bar and the two escapees get showered with glass and booze. Marcus hands Miranda his laser pistol. The leader of the M.E.R.M.-Aid unit stands behind the bar and lays down suppressive fire while Marcus works on her phasing chip like before. A soldier hits Miranda on the left arm with a glancing laser shot but she just smiles at the pain and turns his face into a crisscross of gore.

Marcus succeeds in using her phase chip to send out a pulse that takes down the protective force field over the viewport with a flash of energy. The enemy soldiers don't realize this right away so they keep shooting and the window starts to crack – with the pressure of the Atlantic right behind it. Marcus and Miranda help it along by turning around and blasting the cracks open even wider until the cold salt water pours into the room. Everyone gets washed out into the ocean before the emergency force field comes up.

Brendan is in the command chair of the *Surcease*, nervous as hell over how long the mission is taking. His beloved fiancé and his best friend are in a city full of enemies. Josue then turns to him from the comm station and says, "Dr. Kim – I've detected something. A part of the hotel has been breached."

Josue magnifies an area on the viewscreen and they can see Marcus and Miranda swimming amidst a group of floating soldiers. Brendan says, "Let's get them. Quick!" They set an intercept course and surge toward them through the Atlantic City water.

Miranda phases in her flipper and swooshes through the water with Marcus trying to keep up. A few of the washed out soldiers are air breathers and they flail in the water until they drown, their bodies going still and drifting like flotsam. Other soldiers are aquas, however, and after getting their bearings they try to keep the fugitives from escaping. Miranda swims up to one of the soldiers, shoves her hand into his mouth, grabs his lower jaw while holding his collar for leverage, and *pulls* the man's head from his body. Blood spouts from his neck like a party streamer. Marcus has an underwater fist fight with another soldier (they all had land guns that are useless out here) and knocks the man out with a series of hard right crosses to the face. Miranda knows she can swim much faster so she goes back, grabs Marcus from behind, clasps her hands around his chest, and then swims away from the hotel. Other soldiers saw what Miranda did to their comrade so they think *fuck this* and swim off.

Another threat approaches them, however: two of the same trapezoidal sub drones from the New Richmond attack. Drones designed and manufactured by Memnon Industries.

In combat you only have a split second to make a decision, and in that split second the two Unified soldiers assess their options. They can't outswim the drones and they have no aquatic weapons, so their only option is to evade them. They split up and hope to Mother Ocean that Brendan shows up to get them before they're cut to pieces.

Miranda swims out toward deeper water over where the Atlantic City beach used to be while Marcus swims closer to the casinos. One drone zips through the water after the M.E.R.M.-Aid leader while the other goes to play hide n' seek with Lieutenant Taylor. Marcus swims close to a viewport on one of Reef's upper levels, suspecting that the drone is programmed to not fire at a partition with civilians behind it because of the liability potential. The casino guests beyond the glass see a man in a tuxedo being pursued by a deadly, floating robot with glowing red eyes and they start screaming and running away. Marcus's hunch was correct; the drone holds its fire and decides to swim about to pursue Miranda.

Miranda weaves through the water in a random pattern to elude her drone as much as she can. The drone sends pulse blasts at her toward the water but she is quick and very hard to hit. She sees a Ferris wheel on the sunken boardwalk and decides to swim for it as fast as she can. She risks a glance behind and notices the other drone and a pang of terror shoots through her as she worries that Marcus might be dead. No time to think about that now as she swooshes through the water in an evasive pattern. The drones send torpedoes surging toward her. Miranda reaches the Ferris wheel and spirals through the spokes just before the torpedoes slam into the large amusement ride in a bubbling capriccio. The Ferris wheel topples over and kicks up silt as Miranda swims further from the drones.

The *Surcease* then de-cloaks and blasts the two drones with its formidable pulse cannons. Miranda looks at her fiancé's sub and makes a gesture back toward the casinos. She's going back for Marcus (if he's alive), and the sub will have to hold off until she gets him. The city's Seatopia force has mobilized by now and several gray, cylindrical attack subs stream toward the turtle shell-like Unified sub.

The *Surcease* deploys an array of glowing green depth charges and cloaks them. Miranda swims toward the casinos and feels profound relief upon seeing Marcus swimming toward her. Brendan sends an energy net through the water to protect his lover and best friend, sort of like an aquatic smokescreen. Miranda swims behind Marcus, threads her arms under his shoulders, and clasps her hands over his sternum. He's good in the water for a human but she is much faster. Miranda swooshes her flipper as hard as she can with Marcus in her arms and they race back toward the sub.

A few enemy subs plow into the depth charge grid and explode, adding to the collection of wrecks around the city, but others get through to send torpedoes and pulse blasts rippling through the water.

The *Surcease* sends out countermeasures to stop the torpedoes while releasing a barrage of its own – targeting the vulnerable underbelly of the enemy subs. The Unified sub is greatly outnumbered though and a torpedo gets through to explode against the force shield along with several pulse blasts. The sub is rocked and everyone topples over, but Josue hangs on, waits in tension until Miranda and Marcus get into range, drops the shield, and then operates the tractor beam. The beam goes through the water and enshrouds them like a parent's arms as the energy net dissipates, and Miranda and Marcus are pulled into the lockout trunk. Josue reactivates the shield as soon as they're in. More enemy torpedoes are on the way but the *Surcease* quickly cloaks and rushes through the ocean at maximum speed. The torpedoes collide and detonate in empty water where the sub just was.

Miranda holds Marcus in the lockout trunk but then unclasps her hands to let him go as the water level starts dropping, and he swims away from her. Now that they're in safety the guilt of their drugged make out session starts sinking in.

The water empties out of the chamber and Kris opens the door to find them lying on the bottom, exhausted and dripping wet. She puts a towel around Marcus and says, "So what did you find out?"

He catches his breath and says, "They took them to Memnon Industries. New Albany."

Chapter 15

Kephera continues to suffer in Hologram Hell. Yet she resists, with grace and dignity.

Chapter 16

Marcus, Ray, and Josue surge through the ocean in their fighter subs, performing a training exercise so Josue can join them in the upcoming attack.

He seems to be a natural.

They maneuver the small subs over a seascape of stores, houses, and streets like any other pre-deluge American town, and Josue spots the overpass of an old highway with fish swimming around the girders. He goes full throttle and speeds toward the sea floor, zooms beneath the overpass, and rises toward the surface with silt and bubbles billowing beneath him.

Ray says, "Showoff…" into the comm. He and Marcus are thrilled at how quickly their handsome Dominican friend has excelled at piloting his fighter. Ray and Marcus dip beneath the overpass and rise up after him. It's now time for the best part of their training mission: target practice.

The three friends scan the town and their lights illuminate a school bus on the sea floor that's now a haven for marine life. They then notice a long, broad boulevard full of rusted traffic lights beyond the ancient bus. Perfect. Marcus and Ray let Josue lead, and the former MMA cage fighter zooms through the water over the street… then fires his pulse cannons at the traffic lights. He destroys one after the other like a deadeye, causing the lights to explode one after another in a burst of bubbles. Marcus and Ray are impressed again.

They do a few more strafing runs over other traffic light-filled streets, being careful not to harm any sea life, until it's time to head back to the *Surcease*.

The companions pilot their subs out to deeper water, crossing the threshold of a shelf that drops off into darkness. Josue notices a rock arch between two underwater mountains with stingrays swimming around it. He points toward the arch on the holodisplay they all have in their cockpits and says, "I'm going for it."

Marcus says, "Okay. Be careful."

The stingrays disperse as they notice Josue's sub racing toward them. Josue smiles, guns his throttle, surges toward the rock arch... then loops beneath it, rises above the arch, and loops back around to go under it a second time like tying a shoelace. He yells with exhilaration upon completing the stunt and races further over deep water with his friends in pursuit.

Josue has obviously picked up the skills for piloting his sub in the upcoming battle to rescue Kephera and Cassandra. The three of them go back toward the rendezvous point, and Josue can't wait to meet up with his girlfriend Shelly for some long awaited private time – but first they must greet the arrival of Secretary of Defense Gregory Bryson.

The *Surcease* is docked at the Aulis deep sea station, a clandestine facility loyal to the old U.S. government. The station looks akin to a giant floating starfish pockmarked with lights and viewports. Marcus and the others leave the lockout hangar to shower and change into their dress uniforms in preparation for meeting Secretary Bryson, who will be conducting an important ceremony followed by a mission briefing.

The ceremony in question is to promote Marcus and Miranda for their valor in the recent Atlantic City mission (among other things). Secretary Bryson arrives with everyone standing at attention. Jonathan watches the ceremony from the ship's computer banks, like a friendly version of HAL from *2001: A Space Odyssey*, and he looks on as Bryson removes the vertical black stripe from Marcus's uniform to replace it with the connected twin stripes of a Captain. He then removes Miranda's silver leaf Lieutenant Colonel patch to put the "full bird" symbol of a Colonel on her dress uniform. They are now Captain Marcus Taylor and Colonel Miranda Ulmo, and everyone claps in their honor.

Everyone stands around mingling after the ceremony. Miranda walks up to Marcus and says, "Congratulations, Captain Taylor. Be glad your last name isn't Crunch."

"Yeah, well you should be glad your last name isn't Sanders – *Colonel* Ulmo."

"I'll stomp your scrotum flat like a goomba in *Super Mario Brothers.*"

"How do you know that game?"

"My fiancé is a video game geek who's obsessed with the twentieth century."

"Oh, right."

Secretary Bryson then clears his throat next to them. The two freshly promoted officers realize he was listening the entire time, and they both feel as if they just let out a loud yoga fart in a crowded class.

Marcus tries to do some damage control, "Um, can I help you sir?"

Bryson waves over a pretty young woman with short, straight dark hair and brown eyes, "I'd like you to meet Second Lieutenant Jennifer Calchas, who will be taking over Blake's position at the helm."

She smiles and extends to shake hands with both Marcus and Miranda before saying, "You can call me Jen. I'm excited to work with you." She has a cheerful, spirited disposition.

Miranda says, "And we're glad to have you, Lieutenant."

Bryson says, "Lieutenant Calchas here is one of our brightest young officers. She's a genius with mathematics and probability, and should be a valuable asset on the bridge."

Jen blushes slightly at such compliments from the Secretary of Defense.

Bryson excuses himself, moves over to where Josue is standing, and says, "Mr. Velerio, I've heard great things about your prowess in a fighter sub."

"Thank you, sir."

Mr. Secretary waves over a woman who looks to be around twenty with hazel eyes and light brown hair worn in a ponytail. He introduces her, "This is Corporal Dana Patroclus, our most promising young pilot." Josue and Dana shake hands before he continues, "She'll be joining you on the mission, and I'd like you to be a sort of mentor for her."

"With pleasure, sir." Josue starts getting to know the Unified fleet's newest, youngest pilot, and then Bryson directs everyone to focus on their main order of business: the assault on Memnon Industries.

The *Surcease* crew files into the briefing room, with the rest of the fleet that arrived with Secretary Bryson (including the *Myrmidon* and Miranda's aquatic soldiers) watching on holofeed.

Bryson initiates the briefing, "President Barker has authorized the use of force in a full scale Unified assault on Memnon Industries just outside New Albany. Our mission is to take over the bubble dome just like we did with New Charlotte and New Richmond, but this time the goal is to rescue the sentient hologram you call Kephera while ousting the CEO, Dr. Martin Memnon. We don't know much about Memnon, but the limited intel we do have suggests that he's a slimy bastard. We've been looking for a reason to go after him for some time, and now we have one. Forgive me for being blunt about your friend, but if Kephera's program is honed it could be used as a weapon of immeasurable power – and it could be extremely dangerous in the wrong hands."

Jon doesn't like hearing his lover talked about in such cold, clinical terms.

Bryson continues, "So it is imperative that we recover her while also dealing with Memnon. I'll turn things over to Dr. Kim so he can tell you what we *do* know about Memnon and his corporation's unique bubble dome."

Brendan steps to the front of the room, brings up a four dimensional image of Memnon, and says, "Dr. Martin Memnon is a mysterious recluse who is considered to be the world's leading expert on holographic technology, which could explain why he kidnapped Kephera. It's less clear why he kidnapped Kristin's mother, Cassandra Thatcher."

Kris has a shooting feeling of distress upon hearing her mom's name, and Marcus puts a reassuring hand on her lap; she's worried sick about the only blood relative she has left. Kris senses that there's a deep connection between Kephera and her mother, but she's not sure what it is.

Brendan goes on, "Memnon is a creative genius in a variety of areas. Nobody really knows that much about him because he's rarely seen outside of New Albany, and when he does make a rare public appearance he is never seen without his personal assistant." Brendan brings up a picture of Iris, before going back to Memnon's picture. "Dr. Memnon is a member of the corporate council, but he almost always attends meetings remotely via holofeed. The other council members tolerate this because of how creative, wealthy, and productive he is, so he has something like what psychologists call 'idiosyncrasy credits' in that he uses his talent to get away with strange behavior that would not be tolerated in others. Memnon's corporation is also odd in that they're involved in so many different things without specializing in one area, like how Pharmadyne had a near monopoly on pharmaceuticals."

"We know that Memnon Industries manufactures the sub drones we've encountered before – so we should expect to fight lots of them. So what are the city's other defenses like? Well…" Brendan pulls up a holomap of the New Albany area "…Memnon Industries has its own bubble dome near New Albany, but the corporation pretty much owns the city so Memnon will have use of their defense force. The bubble dome that houses Memnon Industries is very unusual, and attacking it may actually be harder than attacking a normal city. Much harder, I'm afraid. For one thing, the dome is in shallower water surrounded by rocks, almost like an old ship graveyard. The bunker that controls the force shield over the dome's main hangar is in a narrow, heavily fortified underwater cave near a deeper section of the city called Scamander. So it's difficult to even reach in the first place, let alone destroy."

This elicits a collective groan from the crew.

"That's not all…" Brendan shows a detailed close up of the lockout hangar, and everyone can see a translucent wall of shifting, spectrum-like colors "…this is called The Prism Gate. It's unique and mysterious, and nobody knows anything about the technology that operates it – but it's believed to be the most advanced defense barrier in the world. Apparently each one of the shifting colors represents a different type of excruciating death for anyone trying to get through."

This triggers an even bigger groan from everyone, and Ray asks, "So how do we get through that thing?"

"I know that you all may be discouraged by this, but we do have a wild card in our deck. Jonathan, are you here?"

Jon extrudes himself from the ship's computer system and materializes near Brendan. Some of the newly arrived soldiers gasp as it's still a shock for some to see this. Brendan knows how shy Jon is so he feels a little bad putting him on the spot, but it can't be helped. Jon says, with a tinge of nervousness in his voice, "I was able to take down the city's force shield at The Battle of New Charlotte, and Kephera and I did the same thing at New Richmond. The *Surcease* can send me into Memnon Industries with an energy tether and I can work on taking down the Prism Gate from within."

Jen raises her hand and asks, "But if we don't know anything about the gate's technology, then how can you know how to take it down?"

"Um…" Jon wasn't expecting any questions so his fear of public speaking kicks in and his mind goes blank.

Brendan helps him out by saying, "If anybody can take down that gate then Jonathan can. He's an expert with all kinds of force field energy. We *have* to get Kephera away from Memnon, and this is our best chance. Any other questions?"

Jon feels relieved by Brendan's help (the two of them have forged a strong friendship over the past few months), and his nervousness subsides. Jon can't really explain how he manipulates force fields, he just *does* it. It's a gift; he was good at it when he was alive and he's even better at it as a hologram. Jon is aching to be with Kephera again, and he's willing to do anything to get her back.

Brendan and Secretary Bryson wrap up the meeting, and everyone dissipates. Jonathan stays in human form to go off with Ray, and eventually the only people left behind are Marcus and Kris. Kris is grateful for his support when she was visibly upset about her mother, but she feels wary about something. Most women can tell when something is a little off with their relationship, and Marcus has been acting awkward around her ever since the Reef mission.

Kris sighs and decides that this is as good a time as any to bring it up, "Marcus, is everything okay? I mean, with you and me."

"Sure, why wouldn't it be?"

"Well… you've been acting strange around me ever since you got back from that mission, like you've been looking away instead of making direct eye contact like you normally do. It just makes me think something's wrong."

Marcus sighs as well, sits back, holds Kris's hand, and says, "Kris, there's something I should tell you."

"Oh fuck."

"On that mission, Miranda and I…"

"Oh *fuck*."

Marcus is nervous and stumbles for words a bit, but composes himself and says, "You know how much I love you, but on that mission Miranda and I got captured and drugged. In our cell the drugs made us… well, we made out for a bit, but I swear we didn't have sex."

Kris has been labile because of everything that's happened, and she was upset to begin with from the briefing. And now this. She doesn't respond to him and looks away with subtle tears welling in her eyes.

Marcus says, "Look, Kris, we weren't in the right frame of mind. We were drugged, and I thought we were going to die."

She looks back at him. "So the last thing you decide to do in life is betray me? With your best friend's fiancé?"

"Look, baby, I told you – *I didn't fuck her*."

Kris makes a sound of frustration and says, "That's not the point! The point is that I've been having a rough time. I watched my mother and my best friend get kidnapped and I was helpless to stop it, the guilt of that is killing me, and I need you now more than ever… but yet you didn't even *consider* my feelings."

"Kris, I…" Marcus doesn't know what to say.

Kristin stands up and walks toward the big, metal submarine door. She looks back, says, "Asshole…", and *slams* the door shut as she leaves the room.

Chapter 17

Dr. Memnon is furious. He storms into the open air observation lounge of his corporate headquarters, which overlooks the courtyard with the Prism Gate visible in the background. Iris and Hector follow like always.

Chad and Liz are sitting on the balcony, and Memnon shows them a holopad with a news story running: there was an incident in Atlantic City and part of the Reef hotel and casino was blown open to the water. The outlaws responsible for the incident managed to escape in a large submarine that seemed to materialize out of nowhere. Security camera footage clearly shows Marcus Taylor and Miranda Ulmo exchanging fire with Seatopia soldiers.

Memnon says, "What is this?" He points at Marcus on the feed and says, "Who is that?" in a condescending tone.

Chad, through clenched teeth, says, "It's Marcus Taylor."

"Yes, it is. And what were my orders?"

Chad just gives Memnon a dirty look.

"I told you to kill the others. Yet one of them just blew up part of Atlantic City and killed a bunch of my soldiers. How many of them did you leave alive?"

Chad says, "I don't know. They had anti-aircraft missiles so I wasn't going to stick around. We got what we came for."

Memnon moves on, "There's something else that bothers me even more." He switches off the news broadcast, and brings up the note that Liz left for Kris. "What is *this*?"

Liz and Chad just look at the note in silence, mortified that Memnon discovered it.

"Not only did you fail to kill these people, but you invited a lethal assassin right to our doorstep. You work for *me* now, so forget your personal vendettas over what happened in New Charlotte. I hired you two because of your experience running Seatopia's most powerful corporation, but now I feel like a parent with two ungrateful teenagers. From now on, when I give you an order you *follow* it. Is that clear?"

Liz and Chad scowl at him in response.

"Is... that... *clear?*"

Liz, with a soft, angry tone, says, "...it's clear."

"Good." Memnon then turns from the beautiful view of the fountains and leaves the balcony to take care of his next order of business.

He walks through his executive complex and goes into Kephera's chamber to check on her. He goes up to the clear box containing Hologram Hell, and smiles at the beautiful ball of light wriggling as red lasers sear into it from all angles in a rotating pattern. Iris stands aside so Memnon can check the status of his elaborate program to determine how much more supple her will is after a few days in there, like a chef checking a stew. He sees where she's at in the program's holographic world...

Kephera is in human form floating in an endless sea of stinging pink fluid, squirming and grimacing in pain. Four wisping tendrils swim near her, wrap around her wrists and ankles, and pull her body taut like a "x". Four dimensional images then start forming in the fluid before her, and she thinks *oh no... not again...* she wants to shut her eyes but every time there's always an unseen force holding her eyelids open. She's forced to watch as her friends die again in the most gruesome, horrible ways imaginable: melting from searing acid, beheaded with a dull saw, sliced in half, pulled apart limb from limb, screaming like animals.

But after the session Kephera feels a shift; she can sense a consciousness controlling things more directly, rather than the random procession of torments she's been enduring for Ocean knows how long, as you lose track of time in Hologram Hell. It feels like she's been in here for a year.

The pink fluid dissipates and she finds herself sitting in something like an interrogation room on an old twentieth century detective show. She's bound to a wooden chair with a table and an empty chair across from her. She sees the silhouette of a man beyond the door's frosted glass. The man turns the doorknob and enters the room. Kephera's heart leaps when she sees that it's Jonathan, yet she's wary.

Jonathan sits down in the chair across the table from her, and she's aching to hug him – even if he's fake. He says, "I've missed you so much, Kephera, but I'm forbidden from touching you. I'm here to negotiate: out in the real world we've unfortunately lost the battle for you, but Memnon has agreed to spare our lives if you agree to work with him. All you have to do is connect with this…" he takes out the Eye of Odin "…and unlock its potential. We can start right here if you'd like, and every second you wait is another second that your friends suffer."

Kephera really wants to believe that this is her lover (she's so tired from fighting all of this… *so* tired…) but she knows better, "I know it's you, Mr. Memnon. I won't fall for your tricks."

The room melts away and she's now in some kind of laboratory with her entire body except for her head wrapped in a sort of coarse cocoon that tightens against her. It's agonizing, like everything in this living nightmare.

Out in the real world Memnon continues trying to aggressively manipulate her core program, attempting to alter it and make her more like him. In Kephera's hell he makes beams of virulent light twist into her exposed head, as her body fidgets as much as it can in the cocoon. Memnon tries to violate Kephera's mind the way a rapist violates a body, but she withholds the core parts of herself from him, refusing and parrying his attempts to alter her core program by holding onto her love for Jonathan and her friends like a heart shaped locket. The CEO of Memnon Industries works harder at his terminal, really trying to dig into Kephera's mind – and she *screams*. Memnon succeeds in altering peripheral parts of her program, but Kephera fights him and fights him and *fights* him to keep her core program intact. She absolutely refuses to let him reach the deepest parts of herself, despite her exhaustion and anguish.

Amidst her screams she yells out, "I know you can hear me, you son of a bitch! I will *never* give in. You can rip my soul apart but I will never break!"

Memnon tries one last surge into Kephera's core program, *twisting* the searing beams into her head as hard as he can while she yells out, but then he's spent, and he withdraws from the terminal in fury. Memnon screams with rage and smashes a table to pieces. Iris just stands there, used to her boss's private tantrums when he has a setback.

He finally calms down, and realizes he has plenty of time to try again – and next time she'll be even weaker. It shouldn't be long now until the electro bitch breaks and bends to his every bidding, despite what she says.

A frustrated Memnon leaves Kephera's chamber and walks to the complex's other side where he imprisoned Cassandra Thatcher. Memnon intentionally keeps Kephera and Cassandra as far apart as possible - he absolutely cannot allow them to have any contact. Hector waits outside while Memnon and Iris go into the cell to interrogate Cassandra and learn the secrets she's hiding behind the madness. They shut the cell door behind them, and lock it.

Chapter 18

The cloaked *Surcease* races toward New Albany in the most direct route possible, while the *Myrmidon* and the *Virginia* lead the rest of the fleet behind them on a circuitous route that minimizes their chances of running into trouble. Brendan tells Jen to open a comm to everyone on board, and he says, "At the risk of sounding like a tour guide, I should let you all know that we're approaching what used to be New York City if you want to check it out."

Upon hearing this Ray decides to look out at the majesty of New Manhattan: the largest and most elaborate bubble city in Seatopia. He feels a sharp pang of emotional pain because his late wife Iphigenia was from here. She contracted a rare, fatal disease that would have been very expensive to treat so the Plutocracy's health system denied her care. Ray fought it tooth and nail but she ended up dying when she was only 29 – a sacrifice of the system. He thinks about her for a bit, but then shakes off the pain to focus on his present life again. He's cried enough tears about that for a lifetime.

Kris has never seen the New Manhattan bubble dome or the ruins of old New York, so she goes up to a viewport and peers into the Atlantic. She sees nothing but open ocean at first, but then notices a giant stone figure in the distance, and Kris gasps as the submerged Statue of Liberty comes into view. The *Surcease* passes right by and Kris can see tourism subs casting light on it as they float around the iconic statue, which is still a major tourist attraction and one of the most popular dive sites in the world. The government tries to keep the sunken relic as clean as possible as a symbolic gesture.

Kris watches until the remains of New York City pass out of view. Marcus comes up to her and says, "Kris, I feel terrible. I never wanted to hurt you, and I want us to get along again."

Kris doesn't like being cold to the love of her life, so she says, "I want us to get along again too, but it's going to take some time for me to get over this. I realize you were drugged, but I still can't believe you didn't even think of me."

"I know. I can't tell you how sorry I am."

She then says, "Does Brendan know about what happened?"

"I don't think so, but that's really up to Miranda. In a way I hope she doesn't tell him because I'm not sure how he would react."

"I agree – it might be devastating for him because he's like a puppy dog with her, but he's so practical that he might understand about her being drugged. It's hard to tell."

"They're both so childlike. He has a constant sense of wonder that's endearing, while she's still learning about humanity, and everything really."

"They certainly are a cute couple, but I must admit that I'm a little jealous of her. She's so strong, so beautiful, and she's a mythical, exotic sea creature for fuck's sake. I can't compete with that."

Marcus holds her tight and says, "There's no need to compete with Miranda, Kris. You're the most beautiful woman in the world, on land or sea, and you're no slouch in the ass kicking department either. You're the woman I love, and I want to be with you for life."

"We might die tomorrow so that might not be long."

"I know. That's why I want to make up before we go into battle."

Kris answers by kissing him. "I don't want there to be tension between us tomorrow, so I forgive you, Marcus – but I can never trust you around Miranda again, and that *sucks*."

Chapter 19

Dr. Martin Memnon stands by the lockout hangar and watches through the force field as a large, gray submarine docks. He turns to Chad and Liz and says, "We're liable to be attacked now because of your slip ups, so I've enlisted the help of an old friend of yours."

Gray-clad seamen egress from the sub, and Fullerton is surprised to see the bald head of General George Ironwood among them. Several top officers follow Pharmadyne's former chief of military operations out into the corridor to be greeted by Memnon, who hired them because of their knowledge and experience fighting aquatic soldiers. They got their asses kicked back then, but they've had several months to study new ways of combating the Marine Emergency Reactive Military Aid Unit.

Ironwood says, "It's a pleasure to meet you in person, sir. I look forward to helping you fortify this dome against those damn mermaids." Ironwood then introduces his officers, "This is Major Peters, Captain Wang, and Lieutenant Rodman." The men shake hands with Memnon, Iris, and Hector.

Ironwood passes by Fullerton. Chad extends for a handshake and says, "It's nice to see you again, George" but Ironwood ignores the handshake and doesn't even acknowledge Fullerton's presence. Chad and Liz fume with anger over the slight; it's degrading to be ignored by someone who used to take orders from them. The officers all ignore Chad, but Major Peters directs a lascivious gaze at Liz's breasts and legs as he walks past her. The unwanted stare makes her feel uncomfortable.

Memnon and Peters walk down the hall discussing possible technologies for obviating the aquatic soldiers, and Chad and Liz look at each other as if to say *we can't take this anymore.*

Later that night the two lovers are sitting on a couch in their guarded apartment, which is essentially a luxurious prison cell. They're allowed to leave and wander around, but only with guards and only to certain places. Other parts of the complex are walled off by force fields. Chad and Liz have to be careful what they talk about because they're pretty sure Memnon tracks and records them with their smart chips, the Eye, or both.

The latest *Star Wars* holofilm is being projected from a fireplace-like station in the corner. The two former Pharmadyne executives aren't paying attention to it because there are other things on their minds, like having second thoughts about agreeing to work for someone who seems more and more like a sadistic, evil madman. Chad caresses his lover's back, and then looks at her and motions his head toward the bed. She silently follows him, and Chad reaches under the bed to pull out a small chest. He punches in the access code, the chest opens, and he takes out two smart chip buffers. Fullerton and Chastain apply the smart chip buffers and breathe sighs of relief. They're pretty sure Memnon can't spy on them now.

Chad turns to her and says, "We have to get out of here. I'm sick and tired of being treated like a piece of shit."

"Agreed, plus this guy is clearly insane - and *weird*. So how do we escape?"

"Whatever we do we should find a way to take the Eye with us. We should have never gone to that Peleus-Thetis merger party in the first place; we should have kept the Eye for ourselves and used it to open a private investigation firm or something. I'm kicking myself for trying to sell it."

"We can't do anything about that now, but if we can get the Eye back and get out of here then we can definitely use it to make money – and be *ourselves* again. But stealing it from under Memnon's nose won't be easy."

They think for a while and then Chad says, "Let's think about the advantages we have… you're a woman, you're hot, and I'm pretty sure Hector is heterosexual. Maybe you could seduce him to get the Eye back."

"Come on, Chad. That's so cliché."

"Well… can you think of a better idea?"

"…um, not really."

"Alright then. Do you still have your knockout lipstick?"

She reaches into her purse and shows it to him, then says, "I see where you're going. I can put this on, somehow manage to kiss Hector and knock him out, and then while he's out we can steal the Eye and make a run for it. The problem with that though is how we can get out of here with Memnon keeping us under close guard."

"It seems like the dome is about to be attacked, so Memnon should be preoccupied. The big problem will be getting past the force fields and stealing a sub."

"Did you overhear what Peters was talking about with Memnon?"

"Some of it."

"Apparently he's pretty good with technology and he should have access to the force field control codes. Did you also notice how he stared at my legs?"

"Yeah, fucking asshole."

"When Jim worked for us at Pharmadyne he used to creep on me all the time. I'm pretty sure I could… um, *persuade* him to show me the force field codes."

"Damn. You're probably in that pervert's slide show."

"I don't want to think about that, dear."

"Okay, so this sounds like a decent plan – but if we get caught I don't even want to think about what that psycho will do to us. I wouldn't put anything past him."

"Me neither. Memnon scares me, Chad."

"He scares me too."

As Chad and Liz plot to steal back one of Memnon's cherished possessions, the CEO of Memnon Industries goes in to check on his other one.

Martin and Iris enter the chamber where Kephera Soleil is trapped while Hector guards the door, and Memnon nods at Iris to let the electro bitch out of Hologram Hell to see just how broken she is. The red lasers retract, the ball of light inside sluices back out into the room, and then the ball of light expands into Kephera's human form. She still has the green collar around her neck. After Kephera fully materializes she collapses to the floor in an exhausted heap, drenched in sweat with makeup running down her beautiful face. Kephera is normally a loving person, but she has witnessed and experienced horrors over the past few days that have twisted her soul – and Memnon was able to taint parts of her program. She looks up at Memnon, looks him right in the green eyes, sneers in abject hatred, and with labored breathing manages to say, "Fuck you… fuck *you.*"

"So have you enjoyed your time in there?"

Kephera just glares daggers at him.

He continues, "You know what I want. Are you ready to commune with the Eye?"

"I would rather die than ever give in to you."

"If you 'give in to' me then your suffering will end, immediately replaced by untold wonders."

"You can stuff those wonders down your lying throat. Jon and the others will get me out of here, and I'm going to kill you."

"Oh, that's right… you haven't heard. Your friends attempted a misguided attack on the city but they failed. I'm afraid they're dead. Their submarines are burned out husks on the bottom of my sea. I sent images from the battle into your prison so I'm sure you've seen them – lived them even, watching as your friends die over and over again. We took Jonathan alive so he's now in another version of Hologram Hell as we speak. If you relax and let me take over your mind then I'll set him free."

"I don't believe anything you say." Kephera pulls her weary body up to her feet, stands up to her full height, and walks over to the menacing device's threshold. She wipes the running makeup and sweat from her face, lifts her head high in defiance, and says, "Put me back in. I would rather be in there than out here listening to *you* and your lies."

He frowns and says, "Very well. You've chosen to suffer. I *will* have you do my bidding eventually – you can only endure so much."

"Try me, bastard."

He nods at Iris, who flicks a switch, and Kephera continues

standing tall and proud as her essence is sucked back into Hologram Hell.

Memnon turns to Iris and says, "Turn it up to maximum."

"Sir, that could kill her."

"I'm aware of that. She's more stubborn than I thought, and it appears to be our only hope of controlling her. Do it."

Iris complies, and the ensnared ball of light wriggles more intensely as the red beams brighten and sear into her with greater force.

Things are much more calm and civil on the *Myrmidon*, where Josue Velerio and Major Shelly Naiad lie basking in the afterglow of their lovemaking on the waterbed Brendan made for them. She nestles against his shoulder in his arms and Josue says, "I've really enjoyed piloting my fighter sub. Ray and Marcus tell me that I'm a phenom at it, and our recent training mission was the most fun I've had in a long time… with my clothes on, of course."

Shelly gives him a kiss on the cheek and splashes the water on her side of the bed with her flipper before saying, "So what's it like working with the young new pilot?"

"I like her. She's quiet and reserved but she's a good listener and a quick learner. Corporal Patroclus seems like a great soldier and I can see why Bryson recommended her."

Shelly's tone gets a little more somber and she says, "I'm concerned about the message Brendan sent after arriving at New Albany. Their fleet is already mobilized and General Ironwood's subs are there, so they obviously know we're coming. How did they find out?"

"I don't know. The same thing happened at New Richmond – it's like the other team has our playbook."

"Are you worried?"

He kisses her on the forehead and says, "Of course I'm worried, but you're the only person I would tell that to. I could never show that to Dana or the other soldiers. This place we're attacking seems weird, somehow – different."

"I have a bad feeling about tomorrow."

"Relax, Shelly. We won at New Richmond, and we'll win here. Ironwood and his idiots don't stand a chance against us."

Shelly caresses her man and feels his crotch, then says, "You're hard *again*?"

"I can't help it – it's the night before a battle, and I'm with the hottest woman under the sea."

The two of them make love again, until they collapse in each other's arms and drift off to a much needed, peaceful sleep.

Chapter 20

Brendan and Miranda wake up on the morning of battle to the *Surcease* being jostled by a huge storm above the surface. Brendan gets on the comm and gives an order to take the cloaked sub a little deeper. The engaged lovers go about their morning routine with the consternation of a day that might be their last. They kiss goodbye, and then Miranda goes off to her soldiers while Brendan heads for the bridge with coffee in hand.

Jen is already at her station with her headset on when Dr. Kim arrives. He likes an officer who shows up early. Brendan sits in his command chair, knowing full well that he can sit in this chair without fear again because of the woman they're going to rescue.

The *Myrmidon*, the *Virginia*, and the other Unified subs streak through the ocean in their reveille horn onrush toward the storm-raging waters of New Albany. They meet up with the de-cloaking *Surcease* to see countless enemy subs waiting for them, including General Ironwood's flotilla of cylindrical gray warships. The New Albany attack subs resemble floating rooks in chess, with torpedo hatches in the smooth turrets and a large pulse cannon in the center.

Brendan sends a message to the fleet, "This isn't going to be easy, but we can *do* this, everyone. Let's go get Kephera."

Memnon's sub drones stream toward them like angry hornets from a fallen nest. The Unified fleet greets them with a fusillade of weaponry, obliterating many in the first wave, but the drones just keep coming. Ray, Marcus, Dana, Josue, and the other fighter subs plunge into the water to engage the drones, picking them off one by one while avoiding their torpedoes and pulse blasts. Shelly orders the *Myrmidon* to open fire on the New Albany subs and one of them burns through the water before taking its death plunge to the bottom. The *Virginia* rams a torpedo into an Ironwood sub, crippling the shielding, before gashing rents in the hull with cannon fire. Dead bodies filter out of the crippled sub like grains of sugar in a cup of tea. Enemy subs return fire and take down several Unified ships in response. A compromised manta ray-like M.E.R.M.-Aid sub spirals through the water out of control until it collides with another and a swarm of drones blast them both to pieces. The Memnon Industries bubble dome has its own array of defensive weaponry that it launches to damage and take down other Unified subs. This is going to be a close, bloody battle – and the sea floor will be littered with sunken hulks before the end.

Brendan cloaks the *Surcease* for a sneak attack, rushes down toward the dome, and de-cloaks right near Ironwood's massive flagship – detonating a cavalcade of torpedoes directly beneath the hull and blowing the big sub to smithereens. He plans to use his sub's cloaking ability to stick and move like this throughout the fight.

Fighters and drones exchange pleasantries near the surface and the flotsam gets washed about in the storm-churning waters. Ray gets tailed by drones so he takes his fighter up below the surface of the roiling sea to shake them. He gets tossed around but they do too, and he regains his bearings to loop back into deeper water then rise vertically like a phoenix with cannons slicing the drones apart. Ray and the other fighter pilots then dive down toward their main objective: the force shield bunker in the underwater cave, dangerously close to the rocky bottom. They dodge enemy fire, but a few fighter subs get picked off. Dying fighter pilots arm their craft and plow into enemies if they can.

As the fighters battle their way into darkness Miranda addresses her troops on the *Surcease* and across the fleet on holofeed, "Our objective is to infiltrate the city, take over Memnon Industries, and rescue Kephera Soleil and Cassandra Thatcher. Half of you will go toward the Prism Gate with me and the other half will follow Lieutenant Triton in her assault on Scamander. You all know what to do. We kicked ass in New Charlotte, we kicked ass in New Richmond, and we will *kick* more ass here."

"Yes, sir!"

"That's not loud enough!"

"Yes, SIR!"

"Say it like you *fucking* mean it!"

"YES, **SIR!**"

"Aquatic soldiers, follow me!"

Miranda leaps into the pool, swims into the lockout room, and egresses out into the ocean with her bloodthirsty soldiers spilling into the raging New Albany seas from every ship. Many drones turn to meet this new threat and aquatic soldiers slice them up with their pulse rifles like peppers on a cooking show. Captain Margot Unagi ignores the small prey and picks a rook-like sub to go after; she swims beneath it, swooshing her tail through the water while dodging fire with adeptness, and then swims to the vulnerable underbelly and places a glowing green disc bomb there. Margot swims away and the bomb blows a gash in the hull, making the sub *implode* and then drift to the bottom. Nearby, Major Lisa Cardita swishes up to a drone, jabs her machete into both of its red eyes, and then maneuvers the robot so that it fires its lone torpedo into a New Albany sub, taking down the shielding. Lisa blasts the drone, making it drift through the ocean as useless junk, and then swims up to sear the now defenseless enemy vessel until her pulse rifle punctures the hull, destroying it in a cloud of frothing bubbles. These women *live* for combat like this.

Lieutenant Ariel Triton and her team swim down into darker water near the perilous rocks, and she thinks about how her best friend Olivia lost her life on a similar mission – and was honored as a hero. Ariel blasts Memnon drones out of her way and swirls through fire-filled water with her soldiers behind her. She sees Ray's team fighting in close quarters and swims to help them. Ariel swims right up to the window of Marcus's fighter, they nod at each other, and streak ahead to battle their way into the dark underwater cave.

Back up toward the surface Miranda swims behind a drone, grabs it with her powerful arms, rips open a control panel, and tosses in a disc bomb. She then rewires the drone to send it whooshing through the water right into the midst of others and the hotwired drone *explodes* to destroy several drones at once in a bubbling chain reaction. Miranda then turns and looks at the faint Prism Gate shimmering at the far end of the force field-enshrouded lockout hangar. It's strange how their target is such a beautiful, mesmerizing mystery. She shakes this off as she sees enemy divers approaching in the battle-filled sea. The aquatic soldiers collectively lick their chops at the hapless divers like a glutton at a Chinese buffet, but then they notice something different... behind the human divers there are women, *with flippers.*

A scowling Miranda opens a channel to the fleet on her shell comm and says, "They have rogues. Goddamn deserters fighting for money - *kill* the fucking bitches."

On the *Surcease's* bridge, Brendan and Jen exchange a concerned look as they hear this over the comm traffic.

Colonel Ulmo plunges toward the rogues with a scornful grin. The enemy divers and aquatic soldiers swim toward each other and collide like offensive and defensive lines in football. Miranda's soldiers unsheathe their machetes and slash the divers to bits. Miranda herself takes out a machete in each hand and beheads two divers with one swoop of her arms, making their severed heads float in a cloud of blood. She then makes a beeline for the rogue aquatic soldiers.

In the command center at Memnon Industries, General George Ironwood watches the battle and realizes it's the perfect time to unleash their new weapon. He walks up to his communications officer and says, "Give the order to open fire with the electro cannons. It's time to mute those goddamn sirens."

"Aye aye, sir."

Back out in the water, Miranda fights an aquatic soldier with dirty blonde hair; she recognizes the traitor from the training lab, and Miranda feels no remorse whatsoever when she parries a blow and stabs through her armor. Then Miranda sees a few sets of human divers moving large, floating cannons into view... and the cannons fire what appear to be harmless, solid bubbles... but then one of the bubbles hits a brunette aquatic soldier named Sergeant Zoe Valvatida, and it *bursts* upon impact – causing electricity to surge out of the bubble like a jack in the box. Zoe screams and convulses as the combination of water and electricity kills her within seconds, with steam emanating from her fried body.

They've discovered a weakness for the M.E.R.M.-Aid unit.

More cannons fire, and aquatic soldiers try to evade the electro-bubbles – but the heat-seeking bubbles follow their targets. Several of Miranda's women get hit and zapped to death, with one getting hit straight on point blank so that her flesh actually melts leaving parts of her skeleton visible as she dies screaming in agony.

Miranda can sense the morale draining from her soldiers so she hides her panic and fights back with renewed valor, yelling in fury with bubbles streaming from her mouth as she slashes enemies to chum. Colonel Ulmo orders her soldiers to destroy as many cannons as they can, but the combination of the new cannons, the rogues, and the human divers makes it really hard and the water is filled with blood and dead bodies from both sides.

Miranda's team continues forging ahead toward the city, but one thing is clear: this fight is going to be even harder than they thought.

Chapter 21

Liz and Chad are in the command center of Memnon Industries as it starts buzzing with activity. They wait for a bit as everyone settles into their battle roles and then Liz discretely leans in close to her lover and says, "It's time."

Chad feels a flush of nervousness in his belly – this plan is fucking crazy. Memnon is scurrying around checking on things (he's a control freak and wishes he could be out there in the water controlling his fleet like puppets) while Hector is alone in the room that's now used for consulting the Eye. He's recording everything as he lets the Eye tell his mind anything useful about the Unified fleet and their attack plan. Liz takes a deep breath, goes into the room, and says, "Hector, I was wondering about something."

He continues focusing on his holopad and says, "What is it?"

She sits on the table next to him and crosses her legs, making sure to show as much of them as possible, and dangles one of the heels from her foot. She says, "I've been around the Eye since it was discovered, but you've been using it more than anyone lately. You and I probably know more about it than anyone, so I was thinking maybe we could combine our knowledge and use it together..." she starts to subtly brush against him.

"Not now, Ms. Chastain."

She gets off the table and responds, "So this is exactly the perfect time for us to combine our knowledge." Liz then changes the subject while flirting with him, "I see how you look at me and I know you want to work with me." He stands up and she continues, "Don't you find me attractive?"

"Sure, but this isn't the right time."

She starts running her hands along his muscular arms through his suit but he stops her and says, "What are you doing?"

She realizes that the plan isn't working so she takes a quick lunge in to kiss him, but he catches her and squeezes her cheeks, then says, "You're wearing different lipstick today..." in a suspicious tone.

Liz decides that Plan A has failed so she resorts to a good old fashioned high heel to the balls. He moans and grabs his crotch, and she leans forward and gives him a brief peck on the lips. She didn't kiss him full on, but it should be enough. He gets sleepy and then collapses to the floor. Chad enters the room, Liz takes the Eye from its case and hands it to him, and Chad puts it in his large sport coat pocket while Liz closes the case. The two of them put on subtle-looking smart chip buffers and then scurry out of the room. There's so much activity going on that nobody pays much attention to them.

They pass the Prism Gate control room and Liz gets a sick feeling when she sees Major Peters in there, but he thankfully doesn't notice her. Liz got the force field codes from him last night, and feels like showering again every time she thinks about it. She uses the codes to go into parts of the complex that were previously off limits, and they head down to the city's emergency exit lockout hangar.

Out in the Atlantic the storm is subsiding, but the battle certainly isn't. Unified fighter subs and Ariel's soldiers swarm around the plethora of enemy ships surrounding and blocking the underwater cave, chipping away at their defenses. They're joined by larger attack subs from above and a full scale battle ensues that turns the deeper water into a hail of aquatic weaponry.

The Unified force gradually fights its way right to the cave's threshold, taking heavy casualties, when suddenly a few holoflaged rocks shimmer in the dark water to reveal hidden tractor beam turrets. Tractor beams thrust out, grab the closest Unified subs, and pull them into jagged rocks, scraping through their shielding and ripping open their hulls to turn the subs into bubbling tombs. A few Enclave subs target the turrets and take them out, but not before several of their ships lie among the seabed's mounting detritus.

Unified subs protect the entrance (with their force shields buckling from damage) so that Marcus and company can make their way into the cave. For a few seconds their lights show nothing but empty water. Red eyes then start appearing two by two, all over.

More and more of them show up until the cave is filled with drones bearing down on them, including spider-like drones tethered to the cave walls.

Josue spirals through the water using defensive blasts to detonate torpedoes before they reach him. He looks ahead and can barely see the shield generator: it's in a bartizan jutting out from the cave's back wall. There are so many drones in here that it would be impossible to battle them all. They have to just get to the target as fast as possible.

Marcus, Ray, and Dana follow Josue by cutting a path through the swarming drones while pushing their piloting skills to the max as they weave around enemy fire in relative darkness; the submerged cave looks like a fireworks display with weapons flashing in the gloom. M.E.R.M.-Aids can see in the darkness so Ariel and her soldiers have an advantage as they curl through the dangerous water. A few aquatic soldiers get blasted by drones and some of them do lifeless, floating backflips through the water, but many others make it to the bartizan with the Memnon Industries shield generator inside. One of Ariel's troops smirks and swims toward it fast. Ariel tells her to wait but it's too late. The generator surges to life, emanating an ominous green glow in the darkness, and then it starts to spin and release depth charges into the water in all directions like kernels in a popcorn popper. Lieutenant Triton's reckless soldier is blown to bits along with other aquatic soldiers, while others streak for cover behind rocks. The cave is filling with silt from explosions and it's getting hard to see, even for the M.E.R.M.-Aids. A few fighters are destroyed when depth charges cling to them and explode, but Ray, Josue, Dana, and Marcus manage to get closer to the target. They set up shop there blasting depth charges to make them explode harmlessly while staving off drones.

The path is now relatively clear for Ariel to swim up to the bartizan and cover it with every disc bomb she has left. The beautiful redhead swims away with her flipper swooshing the water as hard as she can. The Unified strike force turns around to leave the cave, but one of the charges detonated on the ceiling and a huge chunk of rock falls through the water. Ray just barely swoops his fighter beyond it but another pilot isn't so lucky and her mini sub is crushed beneath the rock to be entombed in this cave for eternity.

Everyone feels the blast wake as Ariel's bombs go off and destroy the shield generator, with the bartizan crumbling behind them in a jumble of silt and bubbles. They regain their bearings and plunge out of the cave, but still have plenty of enemies to deal with.

Miranda's team takes bad losses from the new weapon but she orders them to shoot the electro bubbles (destroying them in sizzling implosions) while using disc bombs on the floating cannons. They fight back and gain both territory and morale. Miranda gets the message that the force shield is down so she hurtles toward the city with her soldiers close behind.

They enter the flooded lockout hangar and wait for the water to drain out. There are enemy soldiers waiting for them beyond the force shield just like in New Charlotte, but this time they have an array of electro-burst cannons on flotation stands that look like bumper boats. The electro-burst bubbles can float through both water and air. Ironwood orders the cannon operators who are still out in the water to pursue Miranda's troops and the M.E.R.M.-Aids end up sandwiched between two clusters of enemies, with the water-based cannons eradicating aquatic soldiers from behind in the lockout hangar. The steaming dead float in the draining water, but Miranda orders everyone to stand fast – and tells them to target the cannons first. Their flippers phase into legs, and they stare down Memnon's troops while waiting for the force field to drop. The ominous Prism Gate looms in the distance.

Miranda keeps her pulse rifle out this time, and as soon as the shield drops she blasts right through the soldier in front of her point blank and then blasts through the gaping hole in his body to disable one of the cannons while using his corpse for cover. Margot and Lisa lead a charge into the hangar, cutting down enemies like weeds so they can pounce on the cannons – but many of the weapons fire, and the aquatic soldiers who get hit are shrouded in crackling electricity; they fall to the floor convulsing and screaming in an agonizing death with their legs phasing to flippers. Miranda's women reach the cannons and smash them to bits, blow them up with disc bombs, and blast them to pieces – but many of their sisters lie fallen at their feet. They just keep fighting their way toward the shimmering gate with unrelenting fury.

Out in the ocean the *Surcease* fights through enemy subs and drones while maneuvering closer to the bubble dome. Jen runs some calculations and predicts the best location for the energy tether: an efficient spot that also gives them the best chance of holding off Memnon's vessels while Jon works his magic in the city's computer systems. She pilots the elliptical command sub there and punches a button, sending the tether through the water like a grappling hook. Jonathan suffuses his consciousness into the city, and Brendan silently wishes him good luck. The weight of the entire fleet is on Jonathan's holographic shoulders.

Kristin paces with nervous energy as she feels helpless just like at the New Richmond battle. She looks at Miranda and company fighting their way through the lockout hangar and wishes she was out there with them. She should be the one to rescue her mother, but she doesn't have gills and isn't even a good swimmer. Kris just keeps pacing.

The *Virginia* and the *Myrmidon* close in to protect Brendan's sub just before an enormous submarine moves in to attack the now stationary *Surcease*: Memnon's flagship, a combination pleasure sub and warship called the *Palladium*. It's a beautiful, oval-shaped vessel modeled after an ancient zeppelin; there's a transparent dome on top with a lush veranda beneath it lined with statues of the Greco-Roman pantheon. The sub's beauty is deceptive as it has the most potent arsenal in their fleet, and the *Palladium* unleashes a barrage of torpedoes. The two protective Unified subs obliterate the torpedo array with defensive pulses while returning fire of their own. The return fire is intercepted by drones that rush in to help their lead ship, and the *Palladium* fires another volley of torpedoes – this time directed solely at the *Virginia*. Dr. Gupta's ship can't release another defensive barrage in time and the torpedo wave rams into her bow, crippling the shielding. Drones then sweep in to puncture the exposed hull, and the *Virginia* goes adrift. Brendan watches this with a sick feeling in his stomach because he loves Prapti like a sister.

Dr. Gupta gives the order to abandon ship while playing her last card: homing depth charges. The sinking *Virginia* releases the bombs and they whiz through the water toward their target. A few get picked off but others get through, attach to the *Palladium's* shielding, and burst against the pressure-repelling force field to take much of it down. The *Myrmidon* endures a few pulse blasts from the now damaged Memnon ship but sends torpedoes into the buckling shields to severely damage the suddenly reeling *Palladium*. The flagship of Memnon Industries starts spinning through the water, and many drones and New Albany subs come over to protect it while the crew (many of them wealthy, high level employees) abandons ship.

Prapti's crew races for life pods: small, sarcophagus-like probes that shoot out into the water. Pods fill the water around the sinking sub and the *Surcease* acts as a safety net by pulling them in with tractor beams, but enemy drones float by to destroy life pods one by one and it becomes like a life and death game of *Hungry Hungry Hippos*.

Thankfully Brendan's sub is able to rescue most of the pods, and he breathes a sigh of relief when he sees a shaken up Dr. Gupta among the survivors in the lockout hangar.

Jon decides to go against orders by taking a few moments to search for Kephera. He misses her so damn much and is worried about her like crazy.

Jonathan frantically searches the city's computer systems for any sign of Kephera. He senses a foreboding presence following him through the network, but tries to shake the feeling. He encounters a program devoted to imprisoning a beautiful woman; that must be her. He filters his essence to that program's threshold and hijacks the controls. It's like a miniature, enclosed version of the holonet. He peers in, and he sees the love of his life floating in some kind of cotton candy colored fluid ensnared in the tentacles of a demonic squid that's stretching her body and limbs like a medieval rack. There are also beams of energy searing into her mind and she appears to be staring ahead at something horrifying that's not actually there. Jon knows that the torment is just a manifestation of what's really going on: someone is trying to infiltrate and alter Kephera's core program. He knows his girlfriend, and she will fight it with everything she has.

Jon's heart breaks from seeing Kephera suffering, and he immediately programs a protective bubble around her like a mother swaddling a babe. The bubble repels the nightmare squid, and Jonathan communicates with Kephera's mind.

She shakes off what she was just going through, looks up, and says, "Jonathan, are you there?"

"Yes, it's me. I've missed you so much." Ocean knows he wants to hug her, but if he phases into physical form in there he might end up trapped like her.

Kephera's face then gets somber and she says, "Memnon, I know it's you and another one of your tricks. You're going to have to kill me – I will *never* work with you."

"Kephera, it's really me."

She makes a skeptical look and says, "Prove it."

Jon relays a few memories from that glorious day in The Sacred Place – things only he would know.

"Mother Ocean, it *is* you. I love you, Jon. We *have* to get out of here."

"Hold on…" he tries to get her out but the controls for that are blocked and he can't figure out how to bypass it. "Kephera, it's not working. I've been sent here from the *Surcease* and they can't maintain the link very long. I only have minutes, maybe even seconds. And it feels like there's a dark presence coming after me."

"Jon, you can't leave me in here…"

"I *have* to take down the Prism Gate now – the entire fleet is depending on it. I'll do whatever I can to come back for you, Kephera."

"Wait, Jon - one more thing."

"Anything."

"Memnon's bodyguard Hector has a gold, spherical artifact called The Eye of Odin. We *have* to get it from him – the survival of the human race could depend on it."

"Okay. Love you so much."

She then senses his consciousness slip away; he left the protective bubble intact, but it's eroding by the second. "Jon, are you there?" She knows he's not anymore but couldn't help asking.

Kephera only has a few seconds before the bubble bursts and she's sucked back into endless torment. She feels a renewed sense of vigor from Jon's presence, and that combined with her utter hatred for Memnon makes her come to a decision: she *has* to escape from Hologram Hell. She can't just sit here waiting for Jon and the others to rescue her. Of course she's tried to escape countless times, but she feels different this time. There *has* to be a way.

Kephera uses the protective bubble's serenity to her advantage by welling up every last ounce of energy she has, and turns herself into a glowing bird of pure light. She then perforates the bubble with as much force as she can muster to fly through the shifting seascape of horrors. She fires a blast of energy at the squid and disintegrates it, and then goes as fast as she can – knocking the nightmare creatures aside while ignoring the dysphoric imagery invading her mind. Like a mantra she keeps telling herself that everything is just an illusion created by a great deceiver, even the pain.

She eventually reaches the threshold of this place, a craggy wall that weeps blood and burns like hell to touch, and she turns back to human form. The dying bodies of her friends are nailed to the wall and there's an infernal chorus of anguished moans, but she just ignores it all. She's made it here before but has never been able to get through. Kephera tries to push through again and recoils in burning pain. She then recalls a thought she just had: pain is an illusion too. It feels real, but pain itself won't kill her.

Kephera decides to not let the pain bother her, and uses her considerable strength to pull rocks from the wall as she feels and hears her hands sizzling. The anguished moans get louder and melting, zombie-like creatures with Easter Island heads and disgusting transparent bodies rise from the ground to stop her. Kephera turns around and sweeps them away with a wave of energy. They keep coming, but she keeps working – pulling off rock after rock. She eventually sees an opening, and as a horde of the melting creatures grabs her and tries to rip her apart she turns into energy, suffuses herself into the opening, and then turns back into the golden bird – expanding herself and clearing the rocks away with broad sweeps of her powerful wings. She sees the glass of the lantern-like box, and can see into the chamber. It looks huge from her perspective. The creatures keep coming at her and she feels excruciating burning all over her body, but she's *so* close. Kephera spreads her wings as wide as possible, radiates with ebullient power, and then *smashes* them forward while driving her beak into the glass – and Kephera Helen Soleil *bursts* out of Hologram Hell.

Chapter 22

An angry Hector wakes up in the Eye of Odin consultation room. He pulls himself to his feet, looks inside the case, and sees that the Eye is missing. He rushes out of the room with the empty case and his holopad, but is accosted by Memnon and his usual coterie of assistants. Hector's boss says, "What took you so long? I need that information."

"Sorry, sir – it's all here on this pad."

Memnon takes the pad and gives Hector a funny look; it's unlike his usually reliable bodyguard to take forever on an assignment, especially during an attack like this.

Hector then hurries down to the emergency exit hangar via Memnon's private, executive elevator. He *has* to recover the Eye because it'll be his ass if he loses it. Dr. Martin Memnon is not someone you want to cross, or disappoint.

Liz and Chad reach a long corridor with the escape hangar at the end. She takes off her heels to run faster while Chad takes down the force fields and the two lovers hurry down the hall.

They get toward the end and Liz drops one of her expensive shoes so she stops to pick it up while Chad uses one of their stolen codes to open the hangar, but then a humming force field goes up between them. Somebody must have detected them. Liz tries to get through the force field but pulls her hand back from shock. Chad tries using the code again but it doesn't work anymore, and they panic. She's blocked out, and can't go with him.

Chad looks at her through the energy barrier and says, "We have no choice – I have to leave with the Eye. Run and hide somewhere from that big asshole, and I'll use the Eye to come back and get you somehow. I love you, Liz."

"You know I've loved you since college, Chad. Be careful." She says this just as Hector appears at the end of the corridor. He sees

Chad and starts running down the hall with a frightening look on his face. Liz ducks off into a side passage; Hector ignores her and keeps going after Fullerton.

Chad shuts and secures the hangar door behind him to buy a few seconds. The room has many small, personal pleasure subs. They look like elongated underwater Jet Skis that people ride crouched forward like a "crotch rocket" motorcycle. He takes out the Eye and thinks about how to commandeer and operate one of them, and the Eye tells him with Hector pounding on the door and trying to override the lock. Chad gets inside one of the watercraft, maneuvers it to a one way emergency exit tube, and then egresses out into the ocean. Hector enters the hangar and gets into his own personal watercraft – which is mounted with pulse cannons.

Jonathan traverses the very strange Memnon Industries network and encounters the Prism Gate's program. Jon tries what's worked before on other force fields, but this program is unlike anything he's ever encountered – it's like something designed by Salvador Dali, M.C. Escher, and Lex Luthor if they all dropped acid together during a psychotic break. The Prism Gate isn't really a force field in the traditional sense. It seems organic, as if it's alive. It's just plain *weird*, and Jon can't figure it out. He starts panicking but forces himself to regain his composure because he knows what's at stake.

The dark presence Jon sensed before is back, and he knows it's after him. Jon has to move his core program around the network to avoid it in an electronic game of hide and seek while continuing to work on cracking an extremely complex code he can barely understand. This is by far the most difficult thing he's ever attempted, like Michelangelo trying to paint the Sistine Chapel ceiling in two minutes on a rickety scaffold with someone trying to kill him.

Jon concentrates so hard that he forgets to move, and the presence *catches* him. Jonathan feels a surge of energy, and it's the worst pain he's ever felt in either of his lives. He would scream if he could. He senses his core program being invaded and fried from within, and if he dies in this form then there's no coming back. Jon is forced to extricate himself back to the *Surcease*.

Jon's body materializes on the bridge and he immediately slumps into a chair with his head in his hands. He failed, and he'll never forgive himself. The woman he loves is still back there literally enduring hell, and he couldn't save her.

It's obvious from Jon's body language that he was unable to take down the gate. Jen is a perfectionist and she can't help giving him a subtle look of disappointment. The entire fleet busted their asses and many died to give Jon his chance, and he couldn't do it. Brendan puts a reassuring hand on Jon's shoulder; he knows that Jon did his absolute best, and they don't know enough about the Prism Gate to know what they're up against.

The aquatic soldiers in the main hangar don't know any of this as they fight their way right up to the multicolored barrier, leaving a trail of dead enemies behind them. They stand before the gate impatiently and Miranda thinks *come on…*

All of a sudden the blue section thrusts out a beam of light, grabs a blonde aquatic soldier, and pulls her in. The soldier screams as the blue light makes her skin crackle with electricity and fries her down to the bone until she's just a smoldering skeleton with a charred flipper. Then a beam shoots out from the red section and grabs Captain Unagi. Miranda yells out, "No!" but she can only stand and watch as Margot is pulled into the redness and then her flesh actually starts melting from her body as she emits guttural screams of dying agony. One of Miranda's best friends and top officers, who was going to be a bridesmaid at her wedding, falls to the floor as a twisted, melted pile of bones.

Other aquatic soldiers suffer similar fates, with another being pulled into the green section and slowly disintegrated with acid. Miranda hears the screams of her troops all around her so she's forced to shut her eyes in despair and utter the one word she thought she would never, ever say: "Retreat… aquatic soldiers, RETREAT!" The Marine Emergency Reactive Military Aid Unit thought they were invincible, but they actually just *lost* a battle for the first time.

Her soldiers look at her in disbelief, but Miranda says it again, "You heard me – *retreat!*"

They follow her orders and the surviving members of Miranda's unit go back out to the water, continuing to fight the cannons, human divers, rogues, and drones. Many of her sisters are blasted and killed in the water as they swim for the lockout trunk of any nearby sub. Miranda sees the *Surcease* and races for her fiancé's vessel. A rogue aquatic soldier shoots an electro-bubble at her and Miranda blasts it with her rifle, but then Miranda turns and sneers in derision as she sees a rogue with curly, dark hair swimming right in her way. Sergeant Wendy Wrasse. Wendy fired an electro-bubble before Miranda noticed and she only has a split second to react... Miranda slices at the bubble with a machete but only glances it and most of it breaks off and connects against the lower half of her body. Miranda is engulfed in crackling electricity and she screams in the water with steam emanating from her.

At this point the fighters and Ariel's team return from their successful mission in deeper water to see aquatic soldiers swimming *away* from the city, which gives them a bad feeling.

Marcus looks out his viewport and sees Miranda hit by the electro burst from Wendy Wrasse. He yells, "Miranda!" and quickly straps on his underwater jet pack while getting ready to eject. Marcus arms his sub and programs it to collide into the nearest Ironwood sub, and then he goes back into the lockout coffin. Marcus egresses out into the shockingly cold water but recovers to zoom toward Miranda as quickly as he can. She's drifting in the water and convulsing while Wendy Wrasse guts a nearby M.E.R.M.-Aid soldier with her machete. Marcus grabs Miranda, holds her tight in his arms, and then rockets toward the *Surcease's* lockout hanger until a tractor beam grabs them both and pulls them in.

A few moments later Marcus emerges dripping wet from the lockout room with Miranda in his arms. Miranda convulses against his body with her tail dangling over his elbow. Kris doesn't like seeing Miranda in her man's arms but she understands the dire circumstance and is terrified about losing her, as is everyone else. Dr. Gupta is still stunned from losing her beloved sub and almost half her crew but she snaps into the moment and quickly leads them both to the infirmary. Prapti rushes in barking orders to her medical staff while Marcus lays Miranda's shuddering body on a bed and then gets out of the way so medics can work on stabilizing her. Brendan tries to go in but Prapti stops him and says, "I know you want to be in here with her but we can't have any distractions. I'm sorry." She squeezes her friend's hand.

As Prapti shuts the door Brendan sees Miranda's readouts go flatline amidst a loud beeping sound.

Chapter 23

Kephera changes back into human form and collapses to the floor, finally free from Hologram Hell. She brushes hair over her left ear as she lies there heaving with exhaustion. Kephera struggles up to her feet and then gets her bearings. She will never fully get over the experience she just had, but she has no time to deal with it now. That psycho might come for her any minute.

She decides to rescue Cassandra, but doesn't have a portable holoprojector for leaving this room in human form. She looks around, and decides to just invent one. Kephera gathers up equipment in the room and parts of her shattered prison and then uses her genius mind to invent a makeshift arm band that can project her human form wherever she goes, even places without holonet access or computer circuitry. She uses her former slave collar as the arm band (which she wears on the upper part of her left arm), realizing the irony of using a symbol of her imprisonment to gain freedom.

Kephera suffuses her consciousness into the city's system to determine where Cassandra is, and then leaves both the chamber and her suffering behind to navigate Memnon Industries.

Kephera wanders the corridors for a while, occasionally avoiding soldiers or employees, and then looks around a corner to see a dark haired woman scurrying down the hall in stocking feet with an expensive pair of high heels in hand.

Elizabeth Chastain stops, and the two of them make the most awkward eye contact of their lives.

Liz then smirks and starts walking toward Kephera.

Kephera puts her hands up in an *I'm not interested* gesture and says, "Oh no. I don't want anything to do with you."

Liz walks up to her and says (trying to hide her desperation and not succeeding), "You're Kephera, right? We *have* to help each other – Memnon is a madman and we need to get out of here."

"I can take care of myself thank you very much. Leave me

alone."

"Please. I have the force field codes so I can help you."

"I don't need them. I can override almost any code within seconds."

"So you're not going to help me?"

"Hmmm… let's see… you *kidnapped* me, you tried to execute my best friend's boyfriend, you started a false rumor that my boyfriend murdered me, you fed my boyfriend's dead body to killer sharks… should I continue?"

"I wasn't personally responsible for most of those things."

Kephera lets out a frustrated sigh; she's not even going to respond to such an ignorant statement. The golden beauty then turns and starts walking away.

Liz calls out after her, "You can't just leave me to get captured by Memnon."

Kephera turns and says, "Look. I just spent the last few days *literally* going through Hell. Literally. I'm in no mood to put up with your crap. You and I are en-e-mies." She emphasizes each syllable to drive the point home. "Got it? Now leave me alone, you're wasting my time."

Liz tries one more desperate plea, "You said he put you through Hell, so you know what he's capable of. I'm no saint but I'm nothing compared to him. You'll never forgive yourself if you let him torture me."

She's good, and she knows how to push someone's buttons. It's true that Kephera would feel guilty if Memnon tortured Liz. Liz probably doesn't even know just how evil he really is – he could come up with torments for a human that would make Torquemada seem like a bumbling amateur. Kephera sighs again and says, "Very well – I'll protect you, but know that I could kill you with a flick of my pinkie if you get out of line."

Liz says, "Thank you…" and holds Kephera's hand.

Kephera pulls her hand away like it was zapped, and then says, "Sorry about this, Liz, but since I don't trust you…" she then clocks Liz across the pretty face with a right cross, knocking her out cold.

Kephera picks up her limp body, slings it over her shoulder, and goes off to find Cassandra Thatcher.

Kephera Soleil and the unconscious Liz Chastain wind through the executive complex. They occasionally run into Memnon's lackeys and Kephera avoids them by using her abilities to blend both of them against the wall like chameleons. They finally reach Cassandra's cell, which is guarded by two gray-clad soldiers. Kephera tries zapping their smart chips, but they don't have them – just as she suspected. Memnon knew Kephera would come here if she escaped. She'll just have to take them out the old school way. Kephera, with Liz still slung over her shoulder, turns parts of her body into a glowing blur and knocks out the guards before they can even unholster their weapons.

Kephera lays Liz on the ground and slaps her until she comes to. Kephera then surges energy from her hands into the locked computer panel beside the door. She tries bypassing the code like she normally does but this one is hard – it's unlike anything she's encountered before. She relaxes, lets her intuition guide her, and eventually opens the lock and then the door.

Cassandra is sitting in a room similar to Chad and Liz's but smaller. Memnon wanted to keep her comfortable, and she thankfully seems unharmed – physically at least.

Kristin's mother acts startled at first, but her startled expression is replaced by a look of joy upon recognizing Kephera. She then looks over at Liz Chastain and gives Kephera a puzzled look as if to say *what's* she *doing here?*

Kephera says, "Long story, but I'm keeping an eye on her so don't worry. We need to get out of here."

Ray's fighter sub gets hit and the last of his shielding dissipates. He thinks *fuck* and heads back to the *Surcease* before being destroyed.

In the water not far from him Hector is chasing Chad Fullerton in their personal watercraft. Chad is an amateur at driving these things and he's terrified while steering haywire through combat-filled water. He thinks that maybe it wasn't such a good idea to leave the city in this thing during a battle, but it's too late now. Memnon scares him so much that he and Liz had to do *something*. Hector gets right behind Chad, smiles, and fires the small pulse cannons on his vessel. Chad's craft gets hit and he starts to panic when warning lights go off. Hector could have easily destroyed Chad's little sub but only wanted to slow him down.

On the *Surcease* a grieving Brendan sits in his command chair worried sick that his fiancé is dead. He *watched* her die. Kris walks up to him, puts her hands on his shoulders, and says, "If anybody can save her then Prapti can. She knows aquatic soldier anatomy better than anyone."

Brendan puts his hand on hers in thanks.

Jen then turns to Brendan and says, "Sir, there are two new subs in the battle: personal pleasure craft."

Brendan says, "What?" in bewilderment.

Jen looks at her readings and says, "The lead sub is damaged and I can't get a reading on the pilot's smart chip, but the one in pursuit is Hector Ramos, Dr. Memnon's personal bodyguard."

Jonathan perks up upon hearing this and says, "Jen, do we have any fighters near them?"

She looks and says, "Josue and Dana are close by."

"Patch me through to Josue."

Jen looks back at Brendan and he says, "Do it."

She hails Josue, hands her headset to Jon, and Jon says, "Josue? There are two personal watercraft near you. One of them has a gold, spherical object - you *must* obtain that thing at all costs. The future of humanity could depend on it."

"I hear you, Jon. Velerio out."

Brendan looks at his friend in abject confusion.

Chad knows he can't get far, and he sees a huge sub floating adrift yet still buoyant and relatively intact: the *Palladium*. Chad heads for Memnon's crippled flagship and gets pulled in by a tractor beam. Hector follows him with Dana and Josue's fighter subs close behind.

Fullerton's damaged pleasure craft plunges into one of the *Palladium's* lockout hangars, with Hector's arriving shortly after. Chad waits for the water to drain out with his mind racing about how to get away from a huge man who's likely about to kill him. Chad pops open his sub just as the water goes below the cockpit, and then leaps out with the Eye in his pocket. He winces as his dress shoes plunge into the cold water, and sloshes over to the entryway. Hector *pops* open his roof, stands up, and aims his laser pistol toward Fullerton. Chad ducks behind another small pleasure sub in the hangar. Hector fires but the laser blast zings against the sub. It was a warning shot more than anything. Memnon's bodyguard grimaces as he sees two Unified fighter subs being pulled into a neighboring hangar. More shit to deal with.

Chad waits behind his cover until water drains from the hangar, and then makes a run for it. Hector fires again and just barely misses Fullerton, but Chad realizes that the big galoot isn't trying to kill him – if he wanted to kill Chad he could have easily done it by now. Fullerton makes his way into the beautiful veranda full of fountains and topiaries encircled by statues of Greco-Roman deities, and looks up at the battle still raging above the clear dome. He makes a run for it, leaving a trail of water behind him as he's bogged down by his wet shoes. Hector emerges from the lockout hangar and draws his pistol, making Chad jump behind a statue of Hera. Hector doesn't have a clear shot so he holds off and keeps pursuing.

Fullerton is not defenseless. Before he left Memnon Industries he stole a small poison dart gun from a weapons locker, and he takes it out. Chad waits for Hector to get in range, and then fires. Fullerton is nervous and his hand is unsteady so the dart whizzes harmlessly past Hector, and it just angers the big Mexican cage fighter. Hector thinks *enough of this shit* and starts blasting the statue above Chad with repeated bursts, causing a cascade of rubble to topple down on Fullerton – stunning him. Poor Hera had her head blown off.

Hector grabs Chad by the lapels, pulls him out of the rubble, and plucks the Eye from his pocket like an egg from a nest. Hector tucks the alien device in his own sport coat pocket. Chad thinks about fighting back but he's smart enough to know when he's beaten;

he's no match for someone who has killed men with his bare hands. Hector picks Chad up, punches him in the gut so hard that Chad almost shits himself, and then deposits him on the trident extending from a statue of Poseidon. Fullerton dangles from the three pronged spear by his sport coat, and says, "Why don't you just kill me?"

"Because I know my boss wants you alive. He'll thoroughly enjoy killing you nice and slow with your bitchy girlfriend bound to chair and forced to watch."

At the mention of Liz Chad sneers and *spits* right in Hector's face. Memnon's bodyguard *backhands* the former CEO across the right side of his face – knocking him out. Hector binds Chad's hands with his own tie, and then hears the Unified scum entering the veranda.

Josue and Dana egress into the veranda, trying to avoid being distracted by its captivating beauty. They see Fullerton dangling from the Poseidon statue, and Dana rushes over to check on him. Josue follows her but yells out, "Dana – be careful!"

As if on cue Hector peeks out from behind a bow-wielding statue of Hermes and blasts her right through the chest. Dana's face contorts in shock and she stumbles back into Josue's arms. She whispers, "Tell my family I lo-" and then he feels her body go flaccid as he listens to the morbid lullaby of breath escaping her young body. He barely got to know Dana; Corporal Patroclus had such a long, promising life and career ahead of her.

Josue looks at her killer and recognizes an old nemesis from his cage fighting days: Hector Ramos. What a crazy coincidence, and the handsome Dominican is overtaken by rage at the man who took away both his cage fighting career and the young pilot he was responsible for. Josue and Hector point their weapons at each other in a stalemate, with Dana's dead body still in Josue's arms.

Hector says, "Well look who it is. It seems we have a standoff, Mr. Velerio."

"I'm going to *kill* you for what you did to her. Why don't we put down our weapons and settle this like old times? Except to the death."

"Agreed. I will *so* love killing you with my bare hands. We'll drop our weapons on the count of three." They both count to three but neither of them budges; Hector Ramos is the *last* man Josue would ever trust. The two of them simultaneously turn off the safeties on their weapons, flip them upside down in their hands, and then slowly lower them to the floor and kick them away.

Josue says "Knives too." Hector grins, pulls a knife out of his belt, and tosses it aside while Josue does the same. They also agree to remove their boots and socks and take their shirts off to fight like they did back in the cage.

Josue gently lowers Dana's body to the floor while Hector takes his sport coat off, and Josue can see a gold, glittering sphere in his pocket. Hector notices him looking at it and says, "You'll have to kill me to get that, and it's not going to happen. I kicked your ass before and I'm gonna *kick* it again."

"So profound. Did Shakespeare say that?"

Hector just gives him a sardonic smirk in response and the two warriors start circling with their fists raised.

Josue says, "And as the lion slaughters man, I am the wolf and you're the lamb."

"What the fuck are you talking about?"

"It's a quote, you stupid motherfucker…" and Josue takes a swing at Hector. Hector ducks under the blow and *slams* Josue with a rising knee to the ribs, but Josue is fueled by anger over Dana's death and retaliates with an elbow to the face, a hard punch, and then he grabs Hector and sweeps him to the floor.

Little do they know but there are still a few survivors on the *Palladium*, including two security officers who can see the fight on a security feed. The security officers decide to stream the fight live over the holonet for free just for the hell of it, so now anybody can watch. The live battle quickly goes viral.

On the *Surcease* Jen turns back to Brendan and says, "You're not going to believe this sir but Josue is fighting Hector over on the *Palladium* – and it's being broadcast live over the holonet."

Brendan stands up and says, "Show it."

The holofeed displays a four dimensional image of their friend holding Hector down and hammering him in the face. Brendan says, "Mother Ocean…" and everyone on the bridge is transfixed on the fight. Kris, Marcus, and Ray show up to watch with the others.

Over on the *Myrmidon* Major Shelly Naiad's bridge crew brings up the holofeed and she drops her commander's log in disbelief. Her man is in a fight to the death on an adrift warship that's being broadcast to the entire world. She sits back in her chair and says, "Good luck, my love…" out loud as she watches with terror in the pit of her stomach.

In the Memnon Industries command center, General George Ironwood and Dr. Martin Memnon watch the fight like everyone else. The battle was slowing down to begin with because of the Unified retreat, but this fight has brought the conflict to a standstill as both sides stop to watch Hector and Josue's death match. Memnon discovered that the Eye was missing some time ago, and now has confirmation of what he suspected: Fullerton stole it and made an ill-advised escape attempt. Elizabeth Chastain is nowhere to be found and Memnon's guards are scouring the dome for her. Martin is confident that his bodyguard, a former world champion in mixed martial arts, will win and bring the Eye back to him.

Back on the *Palladium*, Josue has Hector on the ground and is hammering him in the face. After pounding him for a while the Dominican warrior decides to work on Hector's right arm to take away his strength advantage. He wants to break his arm, and then his neck. Josue gets up and drives a knee across Hector's face and then lays his arm flat and lands another knee across the outstretched limb. Josue runs his lower leg across Hector's arm like a saw while continuing to bash Hector's face. This time these two men aren't trying to win a match with rules and a referee - they're trying to kill each other.

Josue continues working on Hector's arm, and then sits on

the ground to Hector's right, pulls his arm between his own legs, and leans back while pulling on Hector's arm to put enormous pressure on his elbow. Hector screams and struggles to escape the submission hold. Velerio is trying to lock in an armbar to hyperextend Hector's elbow, but the Unified pilot's anger makes him sloppy so he doesn't cross his ankles right away. This allows Hector to squirm free (with Josue still cinching his arm), roll over and grab Josue with his left arm, and then use his enormous strength to lift him up. Hector is trying to power out of the armbar. He holds Josue up with his left arm, walks a few paces over to a majestic fountain, and *slams* Josue's lower back against the edge of the concrete fountain. Josue yells out and crumples to the ground.

Hector picks him up by the neck and dunks his handsome face into the fountain, but Josue fights back with furious elbows to escape from drowning. Josue manages to stun him and slither free, and then the two fighters end up on their feet circling each other with raised fists, back where they started.

Hector has a sore right elbow and forearm while Josue's lower back is killing him. Josue gets the big Mexican with an inside leg kick, but Hector has a big reach advantage so he lands a left jab followed by a right hook and a left uppercut combination that has Josue reeling. Hector lands a few more blows then shoves Josue back away from the fountain, making the Unified pilot trip over debris from the Hera statue. Josue is busted open from those punches. Hector stalks him like a hungry predator, and remembers how he beat Josue and ended his cage fighting career by breaking his left ankle and fracturing his heel – so Memnon's right hand man *stomps* on Josue's left ankle. Josue yells out, giving away how that spot is still a weakness. Hector smiles and stomps on the ankle again, and again. Josue picks up a big stone from the fallen statue and throws it at Hector, but it barely fazes him. Hector gives Josue a running knee to the face that knocks him back and busts him open even more. Josue is in trouble, and Major Naiad is worried sick about her man.

Hector kicks Josue onto his stomach, looks at the pile of crumbled stone, and smirks. He lifts up a huge rock… and *dumps* it across Josue's left ankle, pinning him to the floor. Josue yells out and frantically tries to free himself. Hector stomps and pounds him all over until Josue is subdued, and then removes the stone from Josue's ankle and gets ready to crush his skull with it. Josue takes advantage of his leg being free though and rolls over to deliver a kick to the inside of Hector's left knee with his good right foot. This makes Hector drop the stone harmlessly.

A battered and bloody Josue tries to sweep Hector's legs out from under him, but the bigger man blocks the attempt, grabs Josue's left ankle, lifts him up by the ankle while flipping Josue onto his belly, and drags him away from the rubble. Hector then cinches on Josue's left ankle and *twists* like opening a jar – putting him in the utterly excruciating ankle lock submission hold, made famous by the legendary Kurt Angle. Josue *screams*.

There are no tap outs in this fight to the death, but Josue will be easy prey with a broken ankle. On the *Myrmidon* Shelly says, "Come on, baby…" as she knows her man can get out of this. Hector twists Josue's ankle like a corkscrew and Josue tries to crawl over to a statue to get some leverage, but Hector screams with rage and pulls him back. Memnon's bodyguard wrenches his foe's ankle as hard as he can and Josue yells out even louder.

Then Josue tries something in desperation. As a guilty pleasure he and Marcus like to watch old professional wrestling vids from the twentieth and twenty-first centuries (with Shelly and Kris making fun of them incessantly of course) and he remembers how wrestlers got out of the ankle lock. Josue musters every bit of strength he has left, screams with fury, and then does a forward somersault while using his momentum to propel Hector forward and escape the hold. Hector's grip wasn't as strong as it could have been because of his sore right arm. Hector flies forward and rams into a statue of Athena. Josue gets up, limping, but manages to charge from behind and bash Hector a few times, then slam his head into the unforgiving stone. The Athena statue holds an actual spear with a deadly point, and Josue smirks at this. He gets a firm grip on Hector's head and *pushes* his throat forward against the spear – puncturing his throat and killing him instantly. Blood pours down from Hector's throat as he twitches in death, skewered like a shish kabob.

The crews of the *Surcease* and *Myrmidon* celebrate Josue's victory, and Shelly breathes a sigh of relief. Dr. Memnon fumes with anger over the death of his trusted assistant while standing in the stunned silence of his command center.

Josue isn't finished though. He looks over at Dana's dead body, and starts boiling with rage. He grabs Hector's head, pulls him off the spear, and then uses his considerable strength to drag Hector's corpse over to the lockout trunk. Josue limps as he tries not to put too much pressure on his sore left ankle. He glances at the Eye on the way, poking out of his dead rival's sport coat. Josue pulls his foe's body into the lockout hangar, and drags him right up to Hector's personal watercraft. The Dominican soldier is so fucking mad that he wants to desecrate Hector's corpse. The back of his watercraft has a pair of tow cables with very large, sharp hooks. Josue, with a look of crazed anger on his face, takes the first hook and *pierces* it through Hector's left foot, and then *pierces* his right foot as well – lashing him to the back of the craft.

Josue starts the small sub's engine, programs the autopilot, and then readies it to leave the hangar. The hangar starts filling up with water, and Josue goes back out to stand and watch his handiwork. Everyone in the Unified fleet is wondering what Josue is doing, but he simply snapped with anger at this man he utterly detested. Hector's personal watercraft shoots out of the hangar with his dead body in tow and swooshes down toward the bottom at a forty-five degree angle with blood streaming from his punctured throat. Hector's dead body is being dragged through the ocean by his own pleasure sub right before the Memnon Industries bubble dome, with the world watching. The small sub skims across the bottom dragging Hector's body across jagged rocks and battle wreckage. It doesn't take long for Hector's corpse to disintegrate as it's dragged along the bottom, and pretty soon his body is pulped down to nothing but chum as the watercraft speeds out of sight.

Everyone is in disbelief over the disturbing brutality they just witnessed.

In his anger Josue forgot about Chad Fullerton. The former

Pharmadyne CEO regained consciousness during the fight, but just dangled there to remain inconspicuous. Once Josue dragged Hector into the lockout room Chad lifted his wrists up to his mouth and used his teeth to pull on his tie and unbind his wrists. He then tore out of his shredded sport coat to free himself from the Poseidon trident.

Right now Chad is hiding behind the shield on a statue of Ares. He decided not to pluck the Eye up just yet, but he's keeping it in sight.

Josue returns from his shocking display of malice and goes right to Dana's corpse. He cradles her in his arms as tears trickle down his cheeks. He was her mentor, and failed to protect her.

Chad then creeps out from behind the shield and *fires* a poison dart right into Josue's bad left heel. He doesn't miss this time. Josue clutches his heel and howls in pain. A sneering Fullerton says, "Fuck you, land scum" as he watches Josue quiver from the poison coursing through his body. Josue Achilles Velerio then collapses to the floor, dead.

Shelly watches this happen and *screams* in wild grief. She planned a life with this man. They had names picked out for their future children. She reaches out and brushes the holographic image of Josue's dead body while crying profusely.

On the *Surcease* Marcus stands on the bridge in disbelief. Numb. Josue won the fight, but was killed anyway by Chad Fullerton of all people. And now his lifelong friend is gone. He was the Enkidu to his Gilgamesh, Moonglum to his Elric.

Kris, with tears running down her cheeks, shoots a look of bitter anger at Jon.

Jonathan felt guilty to begin with, but that look from Kris makes an acute pang of guilt shoot through his core. The folly of his mercy to Chad Fullerton haunts him yet again.

Jon then makes a decision. He goes over to the terminal and starts setting up an energy tether. Jen turns from the holofeed and says, "What are you doing?" Jon just ignores her and keeps working.

She repeats, "What are you *doing?*" but he finishes setting up the link, and Jonathan Briar suffuses his consciousness over to the *Palladium*.

Chapter 24

Jonathan materializes on the *Palladium's* veranda. He looks past a shattered Hera statue to see Chad Fullerton in tattered clothes making a break for the lockout hangar looking like a kid who just robbed a cookie jar. The Eye of Odin is in his left hand.

Fullerton turns, notices Jon Briar, and thinks *oh fuck*. He heads for the door even faster but Jon splays his hands to send a non-lethal burst of energy at Chad that knocks him off his feet. Jon shoots over to Chad as a beam of light and then returns to human form right in front of him. The living water sculpture artist picks his former boss up by the lapels, *cracks* him across the face, and shoves him against the door with a forearm across his throat. Jon then snatches the Eye with his free hand and sets it afloat in the air near him like a Harlem Globetrotter trick.

Chad gives Briar a dirty look as he wipes blood from his mouth with the back of his hand.

Jon says, "Remember our agreement, asshole? I agreed to let you live as long as you never fucked with my friends again."

"I never agreed to that."

"You agreed to it when you went up that elevator with your life, and I'm a man of my word. I'm going to kill you for kidnapping Kephera and turning her over to a madman, but not now. I'm taking you back and we're going to treat you like a human piñata for killing our friend."

Before Chad can even respond Jon jolts his smart chip buffer aside with a little surge of energy and then zaps his smart chip with a bigger one, knocking Chad Fullerton out cold.

Jon suspects that Memnon ordered soldiers here to retrieve the Eye so he works quickly. He slings Fullerton's body over his shoulders in a fireman's carry position, then goes over and hoists Dana onto one shoulder then Josue on another. Of course the human Jon Briar could never lift so much at once, but in their training Jon and Kephera figured out how to boost power from their source to increase their strength when phased in, like turning up the brightness of a light bulb.

Jon whisks the two corpses and one unconscious body over to the lockout hangar, opens the door, and goes in. Briar places Josue, Dana, and The Eye of Odin in the personal pleasure sub Chad rode into here, and then he places Chad in a similar watercraft. Both vehicles are damaged, but Jon downloaded information about watercraft repair into his program so he turns into a blur and repairs both mini subs within thirty seconds. Jon starts filling up the lockout hangar and programs the two mini subs to make a beeline right for the *Surcease* as fast as possible.

Jonathan egresses back to the *Palladium's* veranda and watches the subs make their way into the ocean, hoping that Brendan can get them in time. A few New Albany warships speed in to intercept but the *Myrmidon* staves them off until the *Surcease* plucks them up with tractor beams. Jon sighs in relief.

He then flows back to the *Surcease* through the energy tether, and the Unified fleet retreats to safer waters.

The two small watercraft egress into the lockout hangar as the Unified flagship rushes off through the Atlantic, away from New Albany. Kristin Thatcher waits impatiently by the door where Chad Fullerton's mini sub is docking. Kris opens the large metal door as soon as she can and goes in after him.

She opens the sub to find a groggy Fullerton coming back to consciousness. She says, "So your grandpa tortured my dad to death, huh? Did you think that note was *funny*?" Kris strikes him in the throat, making him gasp, and then she whips out her knife and cuts his cheek in a blinding flash, "We're gonna *carve* you up, motherfucker". The former Pharmadyne CEO yells out in pain. Kris says, "You motherfucker...you mother*fucker*" while beating on him with tears of anger in her eyes. She then grabs him by the hair and walks him onto the *Surcease*.

An equally angry Marcus is out there waiting for him, and he confronts Fullerton, "You just killed my friend, and you sent me to die with the sharks. How does it feel to be the captive for a change? Now my beautiful, talented girlfriend is going to kill you, and you *deserve* it." Marcus punches Fullerton in the face and draws blood. Chad drops to his knees, moaning and holding his sore face.

Kris grabs Chad's hair and puts her knife under his chin. Brendan steps up and says, "Kris, hold on. We can learn valuable information from him – keep him alive, for now at least." Kris knows Brendan is right, but her heart wants to slit this man's throat. She reluctantly sheathes her knife and then Kris and Ray lead Fullerton off to the brig.

Marcus and Brendan go into the lockout hangar. Marcus looks at the mini sub with Josue and Dana's bodies inside, and takes a deep breath of apprehension. Brendan puts a reassuring hand on his shoulder, and then Marcus opens the sub. His heart breaks when he sees the two dead bodies, but there's something else in there: a beautiful gold sphere with small lights on it. It's mesmerizing.

Brendan picks up the object and says, "This must be what Jon was talking about." Brendan and Marcus compose themselves, order medics to take care of the bodies, and then go off to study The Eye of Odin.

Chapter 25

The Unified fleet hides nestled among the sunken ruins of a town called Poughkeepsie, with the *Surcease* cloaked in open water above like a mama bear guarding her cubs. They took heavy losses in the attack and may not have the numbers for another strike; for now the fleet can only rest and repair.

Dr. Kim, Jen, Kris, Marcus, Ray, and Jon sit on the bridge in rectitude as they listen to the casualty list coming over the comm. Everyone feels the anguish of profound loss. So many died in an attack that was ultimately repelled: half the *Virginia's* crew, Margot, Dana, Josue… and maybe even Miranda.

Dr. Prapti Gupta makes her way onto the bridge looking exhausted. Brendan gets a shooting feeling of nervousness upon seeing her, and he stands up with a stoic expression on his face – expecting the worst.

Prapti puts her hand on her friend's arm and says, "…she pulled through."

A palpable look of relief crosses Brendan's face.

"She was clinically dead for several seconds, but we were able to revive her. Miranda is amazingly resilient."

Brendan hugs her and then goes off to see his fiancé, overjoyed that he still has her.

Marcus and Kris wait outside the infirmary room while Brendan and Miranda spend some private time together. Almost losing a loved one makes you appreciate them that much more, and the lovers shed subtle tears of gratitude. Brendan eventually leaves and Marcus hugs him before going in to check on his friend.

Miranda is in rough shape. She's in bed hooked up to medical devices with her bandaged flipper under the sheets, a wan complexion, and bags under her eyes.

Marcus walks up to her, holds her clammy hand, smiles, and

says, "So, Colonel, since you almost died I think you should give us the secret chicken recipe."

She smiles back and says, "I think I know more about extra crispy after what happened to me. Anyway... does your cereal box come with a toy inside, Captain Crunch?"

"Well, I do have a toy that women like to play with, but it's certainly not in a cereal box."

"I heard it's soggy though, like your cereal with too much milk on it."

Marcus is glad to hear that she's her old self. His tone gets more serious and he says, "You scared us, kiddo."

"I know. I can't believe I let that weapon hit me. I'll be ready next time."

Marcus can tell she needs rest so they clasp hands firmly in an arm wrestling position like the warriors they are and he leaves, replaced by his girlfriend.

Kris walks up to the wounded M.E.R.M.-Aid leader and says, "Hey." Both women feel an icy tension, despite the circumstances.

Miranda says, "Hey, Kris. Please shut the door for a second." Kris complies, and then Miranda says, "Marcus told you, didn't he."

"Yeah."

"I'm sorry."

"I know."

"I forgave him, and I forgive you too. Just don't let it ever happen again, okay?"

"Okay. I understand."

"We can't afford to lose you, Miranda. You're our best fighter."

"In the water. You're our best fighter on land, so we make a good team."

The two of them feel the relief of tension melting away, and they squeeze each other's hands in mutual respect.

Jonathan sits on the bridge where he materialized, feeling better about what he just accomplished but still somber about failing to take down the gate or rescue Kephera. Brendan returns from checking out the Eye, which he put in a secure container and placed under guard. The technology is way beyond anything he's ever seen, so much so that it makes the hairs stand up on the back of his neck.

Jon peers out the viewport and looks down to see fish swimming through the window of an old hotel. He worries about what Kephera is going through in that horrible chamber. Jon says out loud, to no one in particular, "She's like the sunrise, precious like starlight." He then lifts up his head and looks at Brendan, "We *have* to go back for her."

"We will, Jon. But first we need to figure out how to take that gate down. I know you must have recorded everything in your memory banks, so I'd like you to analyze the data with Lieutenant Calchas."

Jon and Jen give each other an uncomfortable glance as if to say, *oh no*. Jon feels awkward around her because she clearly doesn't like him and thinks he's weird, and he doesn't much care for her either because she's such a tightass. This is for Kephera, though, and sometimes dissimilar people can work well together by seeing a problem from different perspectives.

Jonathan Briar and Jennifer Calchas go into a lab to connect Jon's memory banks to a computer and decipher the Prism Gate's bizarre technology.

Later, the entire crew of the *Surcease* gathers in the cargo hold for a burial ceremony, with Major Naiad and a few other guests from the *Myrmidon*. Dana's body has been preserved and will be sent to her family, but Josue's family is right here. They had a small memorial service for him, and now it's time to put his body to rest along with others lost in the battle. There are empty probes filled with memorabilia for those whose bodies could not be recovered, like Captain Margot Unagi – whose remains are a pile of twisted bones within the Prism Gate.

Miranda is still in her infirmary bed but gives a eulogy for her officer and friend via holofeed. Shelly already gave a eulogy for her beloved Josue at his service, but Dr. Kim (in an aquatic soldier dress uniform Miranda had tailored for him) stands at the front of the room and gives a heartfelt memorial speech for all of their slain companions.

He then gives the order to fire the burial probes out to the ocean. Everyone watches as Josue's floating casket soars through the sea so he can spend eternity among majestic marine life.

A teary eyed Dr. Kim exits the cargo bay and is accosted by Lieutenant Calchas who says, "You'd better come to the bridge quick, sir. We have visitors."

"Are they hostile?"

"I'm not sure."

Brendan looks out and sees two sets of subs from New Boston gathered off the starboard bow. He says, "Yellow alert" and Jen complies.

Brendan studies the newcomers. There are attack subs from Olympus Legal that look like horizontal bishops from chess with a viewport at the groove and a massive pulse cannon on the miter. There are also subs from Cranium Corporation that look like slightly open mussels with a viewport at the opening and torpedo bays peppering the sides in a symmetric pattern. These two companies recently had their CEOs murdered on a cruise celebrating the merger between the Peleus and Thetis corporations. The murders are officially unsolved and shrouded in mystery, but Brendan suspects who was behind them and it seems like they do too.

Brendan says, "Hail them. Find out what they want."

Jen communicates with her counterparts on their command subs, and then turns with a smile and says, "They're here to help us against Memnon to get revenge for the deaths of Derek Jupiter and Debra Pallas."

Unexpected reinforcements; Brendan and everyone else suddenly feel better about their chances in the upcoming second attack on Memnon Industries.

Chapter 26

Prapti goes in to check on her favorite yet most stubborn patient.

Miranda sees her and says, "I heard Jon and Jen figured out how he can take down the gate, and we're going back to New Albany with the reinforcements from Boston."

Prapti knows where this is going but answers anyway, "Yes, that's correct."

"I'm leading my troops in the battle."

"Miranda, you know that's not possible. You were literally dead for a few moments yesterday. You had a heart attack and needed emergency nano surgery."

"Sure, but I'm talking to you now aren't I? I feel alright."

"You have burns all over the lower half of your body, and that's not something we can just suture. Your heart is still weak from the surgery. You are in *no condition* to go back out there."

"I'm fighting."

"Out of the question."

Miranda sits up in her infirmary bed, locks eyes with Prapti in an assertive gaze, and says, "I still draw breath, and I will lead my soldiers until there is *nothing* left of me. Now either you let me get out of here, or I will *bust* out of here. You and I are good friends so don't make me knock you out."

Prapti sighs. "Very well, but you're taking a huge risk. Your heart could give out during the battle."

"You can't get anywhere in life without some risks. Now shoot me up to numb those burns."

Ray and Marcus lead Chad Fullerton from the brig to an interrogation room, and they meet up with Jon, Kris, and Brendan outside the door. Marcus turns Fullerton over to his girlfriend, but wants to give him a parting gift. He walks up to the man who tried to execute him and says, "Mr. Fullerton… with all due respect, I have *no* respect for you." Marcus then punches Chad across the left side of his already bruised face. Fullerton sneers at Marcus as he brushes blood from his lip.

Brendan turns to Jonathan and says, "Find out as much as you can about that Eye of Odin device, and anything else he knows that could be useful."

"Got it." Jon and Kris shove their enemy into the interrogation room, then shut and lock the heavy metal submarine door behind them. Kris knocks Fullerton onto the table and binds his wrists and ankles to each corner. She then starts slicing his clothes off with her large knife until he's down to just his boxer shorts, exposing his near perfect, cosmetically enhanced body. Jon says, "Do you remember the other part of my condition for letting you live?"

Chad just gives him a hate filled glare while struggling in his binds.

Jonathan continues, unfazed, "I told you that I would make you suffer before you die, and I'm a man of my word. So I'm afraid Kris and I are going to hurt you, and you *deserve* it."

Kristin smirks at this as she stands there sharpening her knife, and when she's ready she grabs Chad's left pinky finger and slices the top part off, carving right through the bone. Fullerton screams, and Kris says, "Have you ever heard of 'death by inches', Mr. Fullerton?" before slashing his left arm, eliciting another blood curdling scream from her victim. "Now tell us everything you know about this 'Eye of Odin.'"

Chad has a very low tolerance for pain because he's lived a cushy life of constant comfort. He answers in a quivering voice, "I don't know much about it. Pharmadyne scientists discovered it in an ancient chamber beneath the Mariana Trench."

Kris and Jon exchange a glance. Jacob Meyer asked Kris about that, and Jon remembers hearing about something like that on the news.

Jon asks, "How does it work? What does it do?"

Chad continues, "It's basically an information gathering tool. Nobody knows how it works because the technology is so advanced, but it… well, it reads your mind."

Kris repeats him, "Reads your mind?"

"Yes. You think of something or ask it something and it projects the answer directly into your mind. And it's 100% accurate – the device has never been wrong as far as I can tell. It's creepy as fuck, but very useful."

Jon says, "So it's like one of those old magic eight ball things from the twentieth century?"

Kris gives Jon an annoyed look as if to say, *this isn't the time for dorky shit.*

Jon gives her a subtle look of apology and then has a revelation, "Did someone use the Eye to warn New Richmond of our attack?"

"Yes."

Kris says, "Why are you telling us this so easily? I thought we'd have to beat this out of you."

"Because I honestly don't give a shit anymore." All he cares about right now is being with Liz again.

Kris takes a deep breath and changes the subject to something more painful for her, "So tell me everything you know about my father."

Chad smirks, "I was a kid and my grandfather told me they captured the leader of the original Mariana Trench expedition that found the Eye's chamber."

Kris is shocked by this. She never knew that about her father.

"My grandfather was a bona fide sadist who makes me seem like Mickey fucking Mouse. He wanted to teach me about what happens to traitors and land dwellers, so he sat me down and made me watch as they tortured your dad." Chad can't help looking right up at Kris and sneering at her as he says, "What Liz wrote about in her note was true: your pathetic father *did* beg for death at the end."

This makes Kris fly into a rage. She hits him, and then slashes him with her knife repeatedly – cutting him to shreds with non-lethal slices. Chad screams out from every cut.

The screams of a tormented man give Jonathan pause. He feels a profound sense of cognitive dissonance, "Kris… wait."

She pulls back her knife like a baseball batter checking a swing, and gives Jon a look as if to say *don't chicken out on me now.*

Briar says, "If we torture this man to death then we're just as bad as him, just as bad as *them.* I promised to make him suffer before killing him, but I can do it another way. I want to try something that Kephera and I were working on before they kidnapped her."

Kristin calms herself down and then reluctantly says, "Fine. But I want to be the one to kill him when you're finished."

Chad interjects, "What the fuck are you going to do?"

Kris answers him with a backhanded shot across the mouth.

Jon sucks in as much energy as he can from the power sources around them, and then he holds his hands over Fullerton's head like a soothsayer with a crystal ball. Jonathan concentrates, and small crackles of energy emanate from his hands to lap against Chad's head.

Fullerton says, "What the *fuck* are you doing?" with a tinge of nervousness in his voice.

"Shut up," commands a focused Jon Briar.

Fullerton then gasps and his eyes go wide as he senses Jonathan's energy communing with his own. Jon is using holographic energy to link his mind with Chad Fullerton's, thus baring Chad's soul and putting him through a psychological ordeal before he dies. Briar probes Fullerton's mind, and becomes more adept at it by the second as he explores further. Jon goes back to Fullerton's childhood and sees a spoiled child, adolescent, and then teenager who had everything given to him by his wealthy family, a path to success cleared for him from day one with minimal effort on his part.

But Jon sees a dark time in Chad's late teens, and he zeroes in on that period. Briar explores Fullerton's memories of college, when he was a freshman at Seatopia University. Jonathan then discovers a potentially embarrassing secret about Chad Fullerton: he has a clinical fetish for female undergarments, which is why he amended the Pharmadyne dress code to require female executives to wear a skirt and hose to work every day except dress down Fridays – adding yet another policy to a long list of Procrustean rules and regulations.

Briar then discovers one of Fullerton's most painful memories, when his fetish became a problem for him one night in college and then haunted him for years. Chad was hosting a big party at his exclusive fraternity during his freshman year. Being eighteen years old Chad did not have a good sense of his own limits, and he ended up drinking way too much, passing out on the coffee table in the fraternity house's main room, and then soiling his pants. One of his fraternity brothers tried to help him, but discovered that Chad was wearing a pair of women's panties beneath his slacks. The fraternity brother laughed and announced this out loud to everyone at the party, and from that moment on Chad became known as "the guy who shit his panties".

Fullerton was shunned and made fun of on campus, despite being from a rich and powerful family, until he thought about transferring to another university. It was the worst time of his life, but a close female friend stuck by his side: a brilliant public relations major named Elizabeth Chastain. Chad and Liz bonded together through this ordeal and fell in love, but unfortunately Chad's family had already arranged for him to marry a woman from another rich, powerful family allied with the Fullertons. So Chad and Liz had to conduct their love affair in secret.

Chad winces while reliving these painful memories. Kris stands back and watches Jon work in fascination.

Jon remembers what Brendan said, so he turns to more practical matters by trying to find out anything useful for the upcoming second attack. Jonathan strains himself as he searches through everything Fullerton knows about the Prism Gate, the New Albany bubble dome, and Memnon Industries... but he knows very little. Shit. Chad was basically just a pawn for... Jon senses a presence so dark and foreboding that he pulls away in shock and breaks the connection. It was like a twisted briar patch of hatred, anger, and sadism.

Jon looks up at Kris, exhausted, and nods to let her know that he's finished. He turns back to Chad and says, "I just looked into your mind and saw your pain, but we vowed to kill you... and we will keep our word."

For Chad the reality that he's about to die sinks in further and he starts trembling with subtle tears. He maintains his dignity by not begging or blubbering, but people revert to a primal state when faced with death so Chad slinks back to the child inside all of us.

Jon clasps Chad's hand and says, "Death is not something to be afraid of. Before you die know that we forgive you, Chad... we forgive you."

Kris gives Jon a look that says *speak for yourself*.

Chad tries hard to hold back tears, and his terror of the unknown.

Jon then nods at Kris to let her know that it's time. She gets ready to slide her knife into Fullerton's body in the perfect spot for the quickest, least painful, most humane death possible.

Chad Fullerton whispers for his mother, and Kristin *thrusts* with her knife...

Jon and Kris leave the room and shut the door behind them. Their friends are waiting in the corridor.

Marcus says, "So, what happened?"

Jonathan replies, "Kris and I have vowed to never speak of what went on behind that door."

Marcus nods in tacit understanding.

A few minutes later, once everyone has calmed down, Jon approaches Brendan and says, "Fullerton explained how the Eye works and where it came from, but he unfortunately didn't have much information about the dome's defenses. There's an evil far greater than Chad Fullerton at work there. And one more thing."

"What is it, Jon?"

"I have an idea."

Chapter 27

A rectangular, black object with smoothed edges floats in the water before Memnon Industries.

In the command center a communications officer brings the object to General Ironwood's attention. Ironwood watches it for a bit and then realizes what it is, "It's a probe used to bury soldiers at sea. An underwater coffin. What do your readings tell you?"

"The probe is hard to penetrate with sensors, but I'm getting a faint trace of someone's smart chip... it's Chad Fullerton, sir." Ironwood is taken aback; Chad Fullerton must be dead, and his body is in that probe. He calls Dr. Memnon over.

Martin looks at the floating coffin and says, "It's some kind of trick."

"Should we destroy it?"

"No, that might be the trick. Don't touch it."

"So we should just leave it floating out there?"

"Yes. We should just ignore it. Anyone who does otherwise will answer to me."

Kephera, Cassandra, and Liz are hiding in a holoflaged walk-in supply closet similar to where Ray and Kris hid in New Charlotte.

Kephera and Cassandra want to connect and discuss the future, but they can't with Liz present – and Kephera would feel guilty knocking her out again. Hiding out with the woman who kidnapped them is rather awkward, but they feel it's the right thing to do. Kephera finds it annoying having to keep a constant eye on the licentious woman, though.

Every now and then Kephera suffuses herself into the city's computer system to see what's going on, with her consciousness slinking through the network as discretely as possible. This time she extrudes herself, phases back to corporeal form, and says, "There's something strange outside the city."

Cassandra says, "The woods are marching on Dunsinane; the bubble's about to burst."

Liz gives her a look as if to say *shut up, crazy bitch* and then says out loud, "What is it?"

"It's a little hard to believe, but there's a coffin outside the main hangar." She doesn't tell *whose* coffin it is because she doesn't want to upset her too much.

Liz gets a sick feeling and goes pallid, but then manages to say, "We have to go. We need to bring it into the city."

Cassandra turns to her and says, "You don't want to see what's in there."

Liz just ignores her.

Kephera replies to Chastain, "Why? Getting to the command center won't be easy."

"I have a bad feeling that my Chad is dead, and his body's been sent here as some kind of message. I have to see."

Kephera thinks the coffin could be a sign from Jon. Checking it out sounds better than just sitting here.

So they leave the supply closet and make their way to the command center, with Kephera using her abilities to blend them in with the background whenever they pass by soldiers. The complex gets more crowded as they approach the main area so Kephera has to use more caution with her companions, but they finally reach the Prism Gate control room.

Liz peers into the room and recognizes Major Peters. She bristles with disgust, but knows it's a good opportunity. She turns and says, "I know that man, and I'll use him to take down the gate."

Elizabeth Chastain enters the room and makes alluring eye contact with the major. He gives her a look of surprise, and orders the other soldiers to leave the room and take a break. He says, "You're in big trouble, Liz. Memnon's been looking all over for you and he's not happy."

She starts acting flirtatious with him and says, "So you've missed me?"

He knows what she's doing and says, "Liz, stop. This isn't the time."

"It was the time the other night. Remember, Jim?"

"How could I forget? Look, I'm on duty. I should report you to the General."

She ramps up her flirting and senses his resolve melting; she knows exactly how to push this man's buttons, "If you report me then we'll never be able to have round two, and three, and four…" she nestles right against him.

He sighs and says, "I don't want to do this but I have to report you. I'm sorry."

She says, "I'm sorry too" and pulls his laser pistol from its holster, points it at his face, and blasts him point blank. She says, "Fucking pig" as his lifeless body collapses to the floor with a cauterized hole through his face. Kephera was hiding Cassandra with another hologram ruse, but shimmers back to human form and leads her into the control room. Kephera pouts at Liz for the gruesome murder, but then suffuses her energy into the controls, takes down the Prism Gate, and ensnares the floating coffin in a tractor beam. She pulls the coffin past the disabled gate and into the city, depositing it in the main courtyard.

Around the corner in the command center the communications officer says, "Sir, you'd better take a look at this. Someone deactivated the Prism Gate and let that probe into the city."

"What!?" Ironwood walks over to the balcony and takes a look with his naked eyes. Sure enough, the coffin is sitting at the far end of the courtyard by the downed gate. Memnon is going to be really upset when he sees this.

"There's something else, sir. The Unified flag ship just de-cloaked right on our doorstep, and much of their fleet was holoflaged as large schools of fish." He checks the readouts and says, "…and it looks like they have reinforcements from New Boston." He turns to his commander and says, "They're right on top of us, sir."

"Mobilize the fleet. Throw everything we have at them." Ironwood then calls Major Peters, but he doesn't respond.

He and some other soldiers draw their weapons and head to the control room, where they find Liz Chastain and Cassandra

Thatcher with their hands up in surrender near the dead body of Major Jim Peters. George says, "Where's the electro bitch?" They don't answer, and Ironwood orders a few soldiers to remove Liz's smart chip buffer, take them to the command center, sit them down under guard, and find out everything they know about what's going on. One soldier remains to put the Prism Gate back up, oblivious to the subtle ball of light floating in a corner.

The Unified fleet, with reinforcements from Olympus Legal and Cranium Corporation, launches a second attack on Memnon Industries. They engage enemy subs and the sea quickly fills with destroyed, bubbling husks nose diving for the bottom. A bishop-like Olympus sub uses its large pulse cannon to take down the shielding of a former Pharmadyne sub, and then turns it into a floating mausoleum with a torpedo. Another Olympus sub gets swarmed by drones and blasted full of holes, eventually crashing into the rocks below. A mussel shaped Cranium sub blasts an array of drones, working a path toward the main hangar, with the *Surcease* and the *Myrmidon* leading the way and taking down enemy ships at will. Memnon Industries hasn't had time to repair the force shield so the hangar will be easy to access – but they still need to take that damnable gate down.

On the *Surcease's* launch deck, Miranda passes Marcus and says, "Good luck fighting the Soggies, Captain." He smiles and watches her run off, amazed at her recovery. He watches her address her soldiers, and feels inspired by how much she loves it, how she lives for times like this. Captain Taylor then joins up with Kris and Ray to lead their soldiers on a rectangular troop transport sub.

Miranda and the M.E.R.M.-Aid unit stream into the water with their usual surge of fury, like a Triple Crown winning horse busting from the starting gate. They shred the waiting drones with minimal effort and take down some enemy subs, but the real prize is the hangar where they suffered defeat for the first and hopefully last time. Miranda winces a little as she swooshes her burned tail through the ocean; there's only so much the meds can do. The pain just makes her fight with more anger and she trashes an enemy sub with her pulse rifle before finishing it off with a bomb. The surprised enemy soldiers finally start getting the electro burst cannons into range, but Brendan orders the fleet to target them and Unified subs wipe them out with pulse blasts. Brendan called a meeting to discuss a strategy for containing the new weapons, and it seems to be working.

The aquatic soldiers and the troop transport battle their way into the hangar and wait for the flooded transition room to empty out. Miranda looks at the row of cannons just beyond the force field, and this time she's fueled by vengeance instead of trepidation. Rogue aquatic soldiers anchor the enemy force's front line. The water is now almost fully drained out, and Miranda's troops phase their flippers to legs. Miranda looks right at a bitchy looking rogue with light brown hair, and they both smirk as they draw their machetes. Miranda has one in each hand, while the rogue has a gruesome looking axe in her other hand. The other front-line aquatic soldiers and rogues follow suit by slinging their rifles and drawing their hand to hand weapons. This is going to be a brutal, hate-filled battle.

The force field drops, and the hangar resounds with screams of bloodlust. Miranda knocks her foe's axe away and stabs right through her throat, then pulls the bloody machete out and slashes enemy after enemy in a lightning blur of fury. Lieutenant Ariel Triton swordfights the rogue in front of her but cuts her down and then uses her dead body for cover as she blasts at the human soldiers and cannon operators. Major Cardita the combat medic stands back laying suppressing fire as she watches for wounded, and there are plenty as the rogues take down their share of aquatic soldiers. Miranda continues plowing through the enemy force like a buzzsaw, and the hangar floor piles up with bloody bodies.

Miranda's troops get through the first line, but the dreaded cannons await them. Marcus pops through a lid atop the troop transport and tosses up a bunch of small drones. When Memnon's troops fire the cannons Marcus's drones draw in to dissipate the deadly bubbles – rendering them harmless. This kills the morale of Memnon's soldiers, and they fall back to the Prism Gate. Kris and Ray lead their troops from the transport to reinforce the M.E.R.M.-Aids, and the rout is on. Kris picks off several human soldiers with well-placed shots while using the transport for cover, and she's thrilled to be fighting again.

A few surviving rogues hold their ground though and Ariel engages a tough looking one with curly blonde hair. She recognizes her from the training lab: Corporal Natalie Conch. She was always a bad seed, and was court martialed for insubordination a few times. Ariel fences with Natalie, and they hack at each other with their machetes in an even contest – matching each other move for move. A stray laser blast from a nearby firefight glances Ariel's left arm though and the distraction allows Natalie to knock Ariel's machete from her hand. Lieutenant Triton responds by kicking Natalie's machete out of *her* hand, but this allows the rogue to grab Ariel's legs and slam her down to the blood-slick metal floor. Natalie straddles Ariel, wraps her powerful hands around her throat, and starts choking as Ariel gags with her tongue flicking out. Corporal Conch leans close to Ariel's ear and says, "You're gonna be 'part of your world' permanently, you redheaded *cunt*."

Now you need to understand something about Lieutenant Ariel Triton: nothing pisses her off more than being taunted with *Little Mermaid* references, so this quip makes her fly into a rage. Ariel threads her hands between Natalie's forearms and knocks her hands away to free herself from the choke. She knocks Natalie off her with a powerful backhand strike, takes a moment to gasp for breath, and then springs up. Ariel waits for Natalie to struggle to her knees and then slams her in the face with a huge knee smash, breaking her nose and making blood pour down past her chin. Ariel holds her up by the hair like a puppet and pulps her face with strike after strike, and then leans in, says, "I've never even *seen* that fucking movie," and *snaps* her neck in half. Ariel watches with glee as Natalie's lifeless body drops to the ground with her flipper phasing in.

Marcus is sniping people from atop the transport and he watched this entire display in awe. He reminds himself to never, *ever* make a *Little Mermaid* joke around Lieutenant Triton.

Miranda, Kris, Ray, and their team fight right up to the polychromatic barrier of death, but Colonel Ulmo orders everyone to keep their distance. She thinks, *here we go again...* as they fend off enemy soldiers and hold their position.

In the main courtyard Memnon's soldiers gather around Chad Fullerton's casket-probe with their weapons drawn. All of a sudden Jonathan Briar materializes by the casket, and he quickly creates countless mirror images of himself all over the courtyard. The coffin doubles as a holoprojector. Befuddled guards fire at the various Jon Briars everywhere, and a few of the mirror images disappear.

The real Jon Briar hides behind a fountain and releases a beam of energy at the Prism Gate; all of his doubles release energy beams as well to obfuscate the real Jon. He and Jen worked together to solve the barrier's puzzle and were able to figure out how to take it down. Jon works his consciousness throughout the network, dodging and weaving around the dark presence like a featherweight boxer. He zeroes in on the puzzle's solution, working fast with laser fire all around his body out in the solid world... and Jonathan takes down the Prism Gate. A laser blast hits his corporeal body and sends him back to his core program, but it's too late.

Unified troops pour into the dome, led by Kris and Miranda.

Memnon sits Liz and Cassandra down on the balcony and points a laser pistol at Cassandra's head. "Where is Kephera?"

Cassandra just looks off in defiance and smiles as she sees Jonathan take the gate down.

Memnon looks with concern at the chaos below, and asks Liz the same question. A grief-stricken Chastain ignores him too as she looks down at her lover's coffin, searching for a glimpse of his body for some closure.

The CEO *slaps* Liz across the face with his free hand then turns the pistol back toward Cassandra, "Very well. I got your secrets so I can kill you now. Your riddles die here..." but right before Memnon can pull the trigger a flash of light surges from the nearest wall and knocks the pistol from his hand.

Kephera Soleil, with an uncharacteristic look of frightening anger, shoves Dr. Martin Memnon against a wall. "I've never killed anyone before, but you're a *damn* good choice for my first." She uses her strength to secure her struggling tormentor, morphs her right hand into a large blade, and *shoves* the blade right through Martin Memnon's heart.

Memnon simply smirks, and starts melting as his body becomes gelatinous.

Kephera phases to light and their forms attack each other with lightning speed like fighting hands in a kung fu movie.

Everyone watches with their jaws agape, except Iris who knows her boss's true form.

Kristin rushes into the courtyard like a kid on the last day of school, picking enemies apart and slitting the throats or breaking the necks of any soldiers who dare to take her on in hand to hand combat. Miranda fights right by her side with her whirling machetes of death acting like scythes at harvest time. Colonel Ulmo sees an enemy soldier blast and kill one of her women while saying, "Goddamn *mermaid!*" Don't these assholes ever learn? Miranda sheathes her machetes, runs to him in a flash, wraps her left leg around him for leverage, grabs him by the temples, and *pulls* his head off like popping a dandelion. His headless body flops to the ground with his neck spewing blood like a busted water main. She looks over at another enemy and says, "Think fast, jerk" before tossing the severed head at him like it's a shirts and skins basketball game. The stupefied soldier actually catches his friend's head, allowing Miranda to run up and slice *his* head off.

However, Miranda was dead on an operating table less than 24 hours ago – and the exertion of battle catches up to her. The M.E.R.M-Aid leader drops to her knees clutching her chest. An enemy soldier sees this, smirks, and goes to shoot her but she sees him, pounces, and runs him through. Colonel Ulmo is spent after this, and collapses to the ground clutching her chest. Lisa runs over to check on her commanding officer, and gives her emergency treatment. Major Cardita leans down and says, "You can take it easy now, sir – we're about to win. You should be alright."

Kephera and Memnon are still locked in a dynamic,

undulating battle of light, energy, and viscous matter – looking oddly like one of Jonathan's water sculptures, only it's a scene of mortal aggression. The humans watching them have difficulty following what's going on or who's winning, but at first it seems like Kephera's radiant mass of energy is overpowering Memnon's glutinous cluster of floating ooze. The ooze recoils from the force of her light, but then fights back with renewed fury – and the swirling light that is Kephera bends back like someone losing a test of strength.

Kephera is only a beginner at using her holographic powers, so Memnon could kill her if he wants to – but his city is falling, his true nature has been revealed, and he doesn't want to kill the woman he covets just yet (even though his best attempts to bend her will failed). Thus, Memnon pulls back from hurting Kephera, morphs into a more gaseous form, and extricates himself into a ventilation shaft.

Kephera phases into human form, looking exhausted, and with a wave of her hand she zaps the weapons away from Ironwood and his soldiers and then binds them in glowing golden rope. Kephera yanks Iris's briefcase from her hand, and frees Cassandra and Liz.

Kristin looks up from the courtyard and sees her mother on the balcony, "Mom… mom!"

Cassandra hears her voice, says, "My daughter…" and runs to the balcony's railing.

Iris has orders from her boss that nobody else should have access to Cassandra's knowledge of the future, so she extends her unarmed right hand, and her index and middle fingers retract like telescope lenses to become a makeshift laser pistol. Iris *fires.*

Kristin looks up at her mother, and her joy is instantly crushed as a laser blast sears through Cassandra Thatcher's chest. Kris watches in horror as the life drains from her mother's face, and she topples forward over the railing.

A grief stricken Kris yells out, "*Mom!*" as she sees her mother's body crash to the stone ground. Kristin runs up to her mother's lifeless body and hugs her in her arms while crying profusely and saying, "Mom… mom…" in disbelief.

Kristin Thatcher then looks up with blood boiling anger in her tear-filled eyes, and because of that infernal note she thinks there's only one person who could have done this: Elizabeth Chastain.

Kris runs up to the balcony with murderous revenge in her eyes.

While Kris was grieving below, Liz was stricken with a catatonic look on her face. She stood up and walked out of the room like a sleepwalker. Everyone was so focused on Cassandra's death that they hardly noticed her strange behavior.

Kris runs up to the balcony thinking *where the fuck is she...* and she's greeted with an empathetic hug from Kephera. Kris looks around frantically for Chastain, but Kephera says, "Iris killed your mother, Kris..." knowing that she just signed the blonde assistant's death warrant – but she couldn't withhold the truth from her best friend. Kris pushes Kephera aside, unholsters her trusty .38 caliber pistol, and fires it at Iris. The bullet goes right through Iris's body with a strange metallic sound, and Iris collapses to the floor with sparks shooting from the hole. Kris runs up and kicks her body, and notices twisted circuitry jutting from the bullet hole.

By this point Ray and Marcus arrive from the fray of battle, and they tell their soldiers to take Ironwood and his cronies into custody. Marcus takes Kris into her arms and she cries onto his shoulder, while Ray inspects Iris's corpse. He says out loud, "An android... a living holoprojector." Ray orders a few soldiers to take Iris back to the *Surcease* so Enclave scientists can check her circuitry for potential clues.

Jonathan is now able to scramble back after being reset and he warps his way to the balcony where his friends are. He and Kephera lock eyes and hug, squeezing each other tight in a longed for embrace. She whispers, "I've seen you die a thousand times..." into his ear.

He says, "I'm *so* glad you got out of that hellish prison" in return. Their hug of reunion is a bittersweet one, as Kristin's mother and many others lie dead.

Kephera then stands back from her lover and says to everyone,

"I know we're all flooded with emotions right now, but we *can't* let Memnon get away."

Kephera, Jon, Kris, Marcus, and Ray rush down to the executive hangar where Memnon's spherical sub is docked. They subdue a few hapless enemy soldiers along the way, and then reach the long corridor leading to the escape hatch. At the end of the hall they see Dr. Martin Memnon in human form hurrying along with Chastain and his new personal bodyguard, Sergeant Wendy Wrasse.

Kris, Marcus, and Ray shoot lasers at Memnon while Jon and Kephera surge toward them as pure energy, but Memnon turns around, smiles at them, and creates a polychromatic force field with a wave of his hand. Jon and Kephera batter against it like birds against a window, and their friends' laser blasts can't penetrate it either.

Martin, Liz, and Wendy all board his sub and the Unified friends watch helplessly as it takes off into the ocean. Memnon's circular sub shoots a pulse out before it and a swirling, multicolored vortex appears in the water. The sub drifts into the vortex, and both the submarine and the vortex disappear – leaving only empty ocean water behind.

Everyone watches this in disbelief, except Kephera – who has known Memnon's true form since shortly after he trapped her in Hologram Hell. She looks out at the open ocean water with her beloved family, and says out loud to everyone, "The creature that calls itself Martin Memnon is the most dangerous entity who has ever lived, and we *have* to stop it."

Chapter 28

Jon, Kephera, Ray, Marcus, Kris, and Miranda explore Memnon's executive complex to discover why he was so secretive. Surely there must be some clues about him and his work here, but thus far they haven't found anything too unusual. Kris has teary eyes because her mother's death is still so fresh, and Marcus holds her hand for support. They eventually come to a secure set of metal double doors deep in the bowels of Memnon Industries, in a rocky corridor close to the seafloor behind Scamander.

The door won't budge, and it resists a laser blast from Marcus's pistol. Then Ray notices a small, polychromatic panel on the wall to the right of the door – it's like a mini version of the Prism Gate. Everyone looks at Jon, and he walks up to the panel feeling the consternation of Indiana Jones before taking the golden idol in *Raiders of the Lost Ark*. Jon suffuses himself into the wall around the panel, but after a few seconds he recoils and morphs back to human form, wincing and doing a little dance of pain.

Kephera walks up to Jon, puts her hand on his shoulder, and says, "Hey, why don't we try one of those moves we were working on before I was kidnapped?"

Jon nods assent, and they stand facing each other. Jon clasps his right hand into his girlfriend's left, and he extends his left palm toward the panel while Kephera does the same with her right palm. Their bodies coalesce and appear as one shimmering entity with only their extended palms decipherable, and energy beams extend from their palms into the panel. The energy flows from them and they waver like the fronds of a mangrove as they concentrate hard, and after about 45 seconds the panel gets brighter and makes a soothing electronic sound.

The large doors start opening. Miranda, Marcus, Ray, and Kris all draw their weapons and gather around the door in a combat stance. When the doors fully open the four of them turn the corner with their weapons pointed. There are a few surprised technicians in lab coats standing amidst holo terminals and a series of large honeycomb-shaped machines. The Unified colleagues switch their settings and knock the technicians out with stun blasts. No need to harm potentially innocent employees.

They walk further into the chamber to discover that the technicians aren't the only people in here – but they were the only conscious ones. There are people shackled to metal chairs against the honeycomb-like machines, with holodisplays above each of their heads showing four dimensional images and scenes – very strange, varied things. The people appear to be sleeping, but they're actually in a form of stasis. There are clear cables running from each machine with multicolored energy being siphoned to a larger tube that snakes down through a grate in the floor.

Marcus looks at a few of the sleepers and says, "I recognize some of these people."

Jon, with a chill, says, "I do too. They're all artists – some of the most gifted and talented artists of our generation. Geniuses who all went missing and are presumed dead."

Marcus points to a young woman and says, "This person here is a famous video game designer, one of the best in the world. She was taken to a hospital with a mysterious illness and was never seen again; people think the Plutocracy forced her family to have a closed casket funeral – and now we see why." Most of the others nod as they recognize this story from the news.

Jon walks up to a middle aged man with brown hair and says, "This is Didier Vander, one of the greatest poets of the past century. I read his work in school and I'm sure most of you did too. He supposedly committed suicide by jumping over the side of a boat."

Kris says, "Or so we've been told."

Jon nods at her in agreement, and walks to the next cluster of people bound in their chairs, "This is Stella Leoni, the legendary Italian painter. She went missing in a pleasure sub accident several years ago. Here is Alejandro Dominguez, the avant-garde holofilm director, and then over here is the virtuoso musician Pekka Reinhardt. His music can bring you to tears."

Jon and Kephera then recognize someone and gasp. It's Trey Morse – a living water sculpture artist just like Jonathan. The media tried to make people believe that Jon and Trey had some kind of rivalry, but they actually had a cordial relationship and a mutual respect for each other's work. Jon and Kephera can't believe it, someone who Jonathan personally knows is hooked up to a mysterious machine deep below the headquarters of a sadistic madman.

Kris says, "So what's happening to them?"

Kephera looks at the displays above each person, and gets an eerie feeling. "These are dreams. These people are dreaming, and the machine is recording their dreams."

Everyone then looks at each other as they realize the disturbing secret of Memnon Industries.

They steal the dreams of brilliant people, and profit from them.

Chapter 29

It's several weeks later, and the Unified fleet leaves New Albany behind with green flames lapping inside the evacuated Troy bubble dome that housed Memnon Industries.

A new, more ethical Memnon Industries leadership now occupies a space in New Albany. From now on they will have to profit from their own ideas rather than stealing them from kidnapped geniuses.

Speaking of those kidnapped geniuses, Seatopia is in the midst of an epic media firestorm over the shocking return of many legendary artists who were presumed dead.

Mayor Priam of New Albany tried retaking Troy a few days after it was occupied by Unified forces, but the ill-advised attack was quickly repelled.

Many top Unified officers are now gathered on the *Surcease* to celebrate their hard fought victory at The Battle of Troy. Jonathan designed a few custom water sculptures for the event and they swirl and scintillate in brilliant, colorful patterns around the perimeter of the flagship's cavernous cargo bay. Jon and Kephera decided to skip the party to spend a private night in their pleasure sub program, and everyone understands because they really need a break after weeks of hard work. Musicians from the fleet play live music while everyone mingles, dances, and consumes food and drink from floating server drones.

Miranda and Brendan are probably the two worst dancers you'll ever encounter, but they practice slow dancing in preparation for their upcoming wedding reception. Marcus and Kris mingle hand in hand, and she looks amazing with her hair down in her blue evening gown. Kristin is somber though from the salience of her mother's memorial service; she has now lost both parents in tragic fashion. Ray stopped using surf after burning down his parlor, but he lets himself imbibe a few drinks as he enjoys the company of his beloved companions.

Lieutenant Ariel Triton hangs out with Lisa and Shelly, but decides she's sick of being a wallflower. She sees the officer she's been admiring for quite some time: a strikingly handsome young man with short, dark hair and bright blue eyes. She thinks *fuck it* and goes up to him, interrupting him as he's chatting with some friends. Aquatic soldiers don't have the greatest social skills because they grew up in a training lab, so they tend to be rather blunt.

He turns to her and says, "What can I do for you, Lieutenant?"

She says, "I've admired you for quite some time, soldier. I think you have a cute ass in particular. Would you like to be my date for Colonel Ulmo's wedding?"

He's completely stupefied for a few seconds, but then gathers himself and says, "...*hell* yeah!" He extends for a handshake and says, "My name is Eric."

She shakes his hand but winces inside because that's the name of the prince from that fucking movie. *Of all the damn names in the world he had to have that one...* but outwardly she says, "Nice to meet you. Would you like to dance?"

He nods and she leads him out to the dance floor by the hand. They start swaying back and forth with hands on each other's hips and eyes locked in mutual attraction. After the first song he says, "I'm looking forward to the wedding, and I can't wait for you to meet my pet crab Sebastian."

Epilogue

Miranda looks in the mirror and checks out her wedding dress while Kephera, Kris, and her other bridesmaids help with her hair and makeup. She ponders everything that has happened over the past few months. They lost Kephera but eventually rescued her, blew up part of an Atlantic City casino, finally took over the Troy bubble dome after a long struggle, and discovered the disturbing secret of Memnon Industries.

She also thinks about all they've lost. Her maid of honor Shelly lost her boyfriend Josue. Margot died at the Prism Gate. Kris watched her mother die, which was like having her heart ripped from her chest. Countless Unified soldiers lost their lives and countless subs were destroyed.

But today is a day of celebration, so she wipes the thoughts of loss from her mind and practices her bride smile. Mother Ocean knows she'll have to pose for a zillion photos today.

Everything is ready, and a contemporary, electronic version of The Wedding March starts playing in the distance. Miranda gets up and takes a nervous breath. It's funny how she feels fine about swimming into a heated combat zone yet has Mothra-sized butterflies in her stomach over her wedding ceremony. Colonel Miranda Ulmo looks at her entourage – Shelly, Kris, Kephera, Lisa, and Ariel – and then starts the most important walk of her life, trying not to stumble in her pesky legs and annoying white heels.

Miranda walks through the curtain and looks around the room at everyone she cares about. Secretary Gregory Bryson is there with his wife. There's a long, vertical pool along one side so aquatic soldiers can watch their commanding officer's wedding in their natural state. Prapti, as former captain of the sunken *Virginia*, will perform the ceremony and waits patiently with a book in her hands. And of course the love of her life, Dr. Brendan Kim, standing up front looking better than ever in a black tuxedo; she's glad he left that damn lab coat at home for one day. Jon, Ray, and Marcus the best man are at his side. When Miranda sees the best man she briefly thinks about the incident between them, but quickly pushes it from her mind.

Miranda makes her way up to the front. The bride and groom hold hands and smile at each other, giddy with excitement. Brendan looks at Miranda and thinks that she has never been more beautiful. Marcus and Jon think the same thing about Kris and Kephera.

Prapti begins the ceremony and goes through a typical wedding speech. Miranda talks about how Brendan has always been her link to humanity, how much she's learned from him, and how excited she is about their life together. Brendan tells her how she's the most amazing person he's ever met, how she's his link to *her* majestic world beneath the sea, how she saved his life at The Battle of New Charlotte, and how deeply he loves her. Brendan then takes a glittering diamond ring from Marcus and slips it on his bride's finger, just as she slipped the ring on his finger back in that magical cavern.

Prapti announces them as man and wife, and the newlyweds embrace with an elongated kiss while everyone claps. Brendan and Miranda then head back up the aisle hand in hand, and everyone goes off to dance and party the night away.

Meanwhile, inside a highly secure metal container in a nearby room, The Eye of Odin twitches to life and starts transmitting an electronic song of ages.

Afterword: Sledding as an Adult

Going sledding as an adult is one of the most enjoyable experiences you can have in life. Now some of you reading this may live in warmer areas that don't get snow so it's impossible for you to *literally* sled as an adult, but I'm sure there are equivalent fun yet slightly risky activities where you live – like maybe paddling a kayak off a waterfall or eating at a White Castle without adequate health insurance. Anyway, you need to meet some parameters before you're truly sledding as an adult. First of all, it's not *really* sledding as an adult if there are any children present or anyone else you're responsible for. You can't fully let loose and enjoy yourself if you're worrying that a kid might fly through the air to end up impaled on a tree like a human windsock. Truly going sledding as an adult typically involves knowing you don't have work the next day while zipping down a snow covered hill with friends who are just as drunk as you are, or perhaps you're a homeless dude whizzing down an icy street on a stolen fast food tray. In either case you're at a place in life in which you can take some enjoyable risks.

At this point let me take a detour on the snowy hill to relate some things about writing the *Seatopia* novels:

-I wrote most of the first two books in my pajamas. If you're reading this and you sit down to write a novel someday then I'd imagine the same might apply to you.

-The idea for The Prism Gate in the Troy bubble dome is based on a *Dungeons & Dragons* spell called Prismatic Wall, which I always thought was cool when I read through the game manuals as a kid. I loved reading those *Dungeons & Dragons* books and looking at the awesome artwork of Larry Elmore. Ignorant people make fun of that game, but I learned many of the vocab words I use throughout these books by playing it.

-My writing style is unusual in that I prefer to write in present tense. For some reason it's just more natural for me to write that way and I like it because it gives the story a greater sense of urgency. I kind of wish more writers used present tense (Charles Stross is a great writer who uses it). I'm also a bit unusual in that I don't write In Linear Fashion. I Typically Work On A Given Chapter Based On The Mood I'm In At The time, and the ending is one of the first things I write. I like to write the ending early on because it gives me a goal to work toward. I love reading (as you might imagine) but one of my pet peeves about fiction is that there are far too many books or series with unsatisfying endings. I like to think of a satisfying ending and then go from there.

-"Where do you get your ideas?" is a question that writers get asked all the time, and it's considered a cliché question that writers find annoying. Harlan Ellison tells people that he gets his ideas from Schenectady, New York. As a sort of preemptive strike I figure I'll answer that question now. I do think it's interesting to consider where creative people's ideas come from so I understand why it's such a common question.

The overall idea for the *Seatopia* series came to me in a series of vivid recurring nightmares that I had while recovering from shoulder surgery in 2014. In one nightmare I was being slowly eaten by a shark but could breathe underwater so it just went on and on. Through those nightmares I experienced how terrifying that would be, and that led to the opening scene of the first book. The other recurring nightmare I had involved the media dragging my legacy through the mud in the aftermath of me committing suicide, which was also terrifying but in a very different way.

As for this second book that you're holding in your hands, looking at on some kind of electronic device, or reading through your smart chip, the idea came to me one night while listening to loud music in my car as I was driving home from a heavy metal concert. I like going to heavy metal concerts and then driving home late at night hopped up on caffeine while blasting music, and one night I was driving home and the epic song "And Then There Was Silence" by Blind Guardian came onto my iPod. The song is about the Trojan War, and the idea for *The Eye of Odin* came to me as I listened to it. I thought about how cool it would be to write an underwater science fiction version of the Trojan War using my characters. Joseph Campbell said that mythology is something that unites all people regardless of culture or ethnicity, and the power of diversity and universal connection is one of the messages I try to convey through these books.

-One question that people *do* ask me all the time is, "How do you find the time?" They're referring to how I work 65+ hours a week for my "day job" and yet still manage to write and publish these novels. There are many answers to that, and one is how I simply felt compelled to write it, as if I had to. The idea for the story came to me and I had a sense of dissonance until I started writing it. That may sound hokey but I'm sure the creative people out there know what I'm talking about; it's how the creative process works, and you can't explain it or quantify it.

Another answer is that writing the *Seatopia* series is a way for me to go sledding as an adult. I hope you've been enjoying the ride along with me.

About the Author

Dr. David J. Wimer is the author of the obscure and partially acclaimed *Seatopia* series, now in its second volume. He is a psychologist and award winning university professor who served as an officer in the U.S. Army Medical Service Corps; all of these experiences show up in his writing. His main literary influences include Harlan Ellison, William Gibson, Michael Moorcock, Robert E. Howard, H.P. Lovecraft, Philip K. Dick, Roger Zelazny, and Brandon Sanderson. He grew up in Washington Crossing, Pennsylvania and has lived in many places including Ithaca, New York and Canberra, Australia but currently resides in central Pennsylvania with a fat, lazy cat.

Follow the *Seatopia* series on social media:

http://www.facebook.com/seatopiasf

http://www.twitter.com/seatopiasf

http://www.instagram.com/seatopiasf

Made in the USA
Middletown, DE
26 May 2017